I0822573

Śrī Śrī

Harināma Kalpataru

First Gem

Śrīpad Aindra Prabhu

I[st] Edition (2018) : 3 Copies

SripadKosh Publications LLP
53, Cedar Crest, Sector - 50
Nirvana Country, Gurugram Gurgaon
HR 122001, INDIA

www.sripadkosh.com
info@sripadkosh.com

Ordering Information:
For details, contact the publisher at the address above.

Printed at Repro Knowledgecast Limited, Thane

Publishing Services by Zorba Books
www.zorbabooks.com

Dedication

As one would hand over a precious gem, we would like to place this volume in the hands of our dearly missed Aindra Prabhu so that he may offer it at the lotus feet of his beloved spiritual master, Śrīla Prabhupāda.

Acknowledgements

We would like to thank all the devotees who have in various ways contributed to this publication, including Dhaval Sachdeva (Vraja-vilāsa Dāsa) for reviving the idea of publishing Aindra Prabhu's spoken material; Sabina Seeger (Sandesh Dāsi) for transcribing the recordings;. Carl Herzig (Kālachandjī Dāsa), who edited Aindra Prabhu's Heart of Transcendental Book Distribution, for editing this publication; and Deborah Rochelle Klein (Dhīra Lalitā Devī Dāsī) for assisting in proof-reading and editing. Special thanks to Roger Tschopp for making the design and layout. We are greatly indebted to everyone who has encouraged and supported us in the process of manifesting this first volume.

– The Publishers, Puruṣhottama Māsa 2018

Preface

SripadKosh Publications is a team formed to publish the spoken material mercifully left to this world by His Grace Aindra Prabhu. A kosh is a treasure or treasury, and Aindra Prabhu was sometimes called by the revered title Śrīpad, though he would screw up his nose whenever he heard it.

Aindra Prabhu's kirtans, writings, lectures, and conversations are rich with profound realizations and a contagious enthusiasm that has touched the hearts of devotees all around the world, and which continue to serve as a source of great inspiration. His presence is badly missed, and his departure left an empty space amidst us that nothing, no one, can fill. Via spiritual sound vibration, however we are able to reconnect with Aindra Prabhu at any time and avail ourselves of his heart-stirring inspirations and instructions.

In the last Puruṣhottama Māsa we observed in the association of Aindra Prabhu, he mentioned that after the publishing of The Heart of Transcendental Book Distribution, another book will come out in due course. It was understood that he was alluding to transcriptions of his spoken offerings. Herewith, we are releasing the first volume of that material: A seminar Aindra Prabhu gave on three consecutive days of Kārtika 2001.

We pray to the feet of the Vaishnavas that we may continue this effort of publishing Aindra Prabhu`s spoken words for the pleasure of the devotees and Śrī Śrī Guru and Gaurānga.

All glories to Śrī Guru and Śrī Gaurānga! All glories to the thunderous congregational chanting of Rādhā-Kṛṣṇa's Holy Names! All glories to the swanlike pure devotees of the Lord!

Kārtika Seminar, Vṛndāvana, 2001

हरे कृष्ण हरे कृष्ण कृष्ण कृष्ण हरे हरे | हरे रामा हरे रामा रामा रामा हरे हरे || हरे कृष्ण हरे कृष्ण कृष्ण कृष्ण कृष्ण हरे हरे | हरे रामा हरे रामा रामा रामा हरे हरे || हरे कृष्ण हरे कृष्ण कृष्ण कृष्ण हरे हरे | हरे रामा हरे रामा रामा रामा हरे हरे || हरे कृष्ण हरे कृष्ण कृष्ण कृष्ण हरे हरे | हरे रामा हरे रामा रामा रामा हरे हरे || हरे कृष्ण हरे कृष्ण कृष्ण कृष्ण हरे हरे | हरे रामा हरे रामा रामा रामा हरे हरे || हरे कृष्ण हरे कृष्ण कृष्ण कृष्ण हरे हरे | हरे रामा हरे रामा रामा रामा हरे हरे || हरे कृष्ण हरे कृष्ण कृष्ण कृष्ण हरे हरे | हरे रामा हरे रामा रामा रामा हरे हरे || हरे कृष्ण हरे कृष्ण कृष्ण कृष्ण हरे हरे | हरे रामा हरे रामा रामा रामा हरे हरे || हरे कृष्ण हरे कृष्ण कृष्ण कृष्ण हरे हरे | हरे रामा हरे रामा रामा रामा हरे हरे || हरे कृष्ण हरे कृष्ण कृष्ण कृष्ण हरे हरे | हरे रामा हरे रामा रामा रामा हरे हरे || हरे कृष्ण हरे कृष्ण कृष्ण कृष्ण हरे हरे | हरे रामा हरे रामा रामा रामा हरे हरे || हरे कृष्ण हरे कृष्ण कृष्ण कृष्ण हरे हरे | हरे रामा हरे रामा रामा रामा हरे हरे || हरे कृष्ण हरे कृष्ण कृष्ण कृष्ण हरे हरे | हरे रामा हरे रामा रामा रामा हरे हरे || हरे कृष्ण हरे कृष्ण कृष्ण कृष्ण हरे हरे | हरे रामा हरे रामा रामा रामा हरे हरे || हरे कृष्ण हरे कृष्ण कृष्ण कृष्ण हरे हरे | हरे रामा हरे रामा रामा रामा हरे हरे || हरे कृष्ण हरे कृष्ण कृष्ण कृष्ण हरे हरे | हरे रामा हरे रामा रामा रामा हरे हरे || हरे कृष्ण हरे कृष्ण कृष्ण कृष्ण हरे हरे | हरे रामा हरे रामा रामा रामा हरे हरे || हरे कृष्ण हरे कृष्ण कृष्ण कृष्ण हरे हरे | हरे रामा हरे रामा रामा रामा हरे हरे || हरे कृष्ण हरे कृष्ण कृष्ण कृष्ण हरे हरे | हरे रामा हरे रामा रामा रामा हरे हरे || हरे कृष्ण हरे कृष्ण कृष्ण कृष्ण हरे हरे | हरे रामा हरे रामा रामा रामा हरे हरे || हरे कृष्ण हरे कृष्ण कृष्ण कृष्ण हरे हरे | हरे रामा हरे रामा रामा रामा हरे हरे || हरे कृष्ण हरे कृष्ण कृष्ण कृष्ण हरे हरे | हरे रामा हरे रामा रामा रामा हरे हरे || हरे कृष्ण हरे कृष्ण कृष्ण कृष्ण हरे हरे | हरे रामा हरे रामा रामा रामा हरे हरे || हरे कृष्ण हरे कृष्ण कृष्ण कृष्ण हरे हरे | हरे रामा हरे रामा रामा रामा हरे हरे || हरे कृष्ण हरे कृष्ण कृष्ण कृष्ण हरे हरे | हरे रामा हरे रामा रामा रामा हरे हरे || हरे कृष्ण हरे कृष्ण कृष्ण कृष्ण हरे हरे | हरे रामा हरे रामा रामा रामा हरे हरे

Part 1

November 27, 2001

Śrīmatī Rādhārāṇī is allowing us to come to Vṛndāvana and be here on this day. So we should make every effort to increase our chances of going back home, back to Godhead in this lifetime. In a verse in the Mathurā-māhātmya Kṛṣṇa is telling that Mathurā-maṇḍala, Vraja-maṇḍala, is not difficult to attain in this world. A brief explanation should be there that if you look in the sky at night, you will see how many millions and billions of planets are in the sky. And it is understood that in each brahmāṇḍa, each universe, there is only one planet that is Bhūmi. On Bhūmi, on the Earth planet – only on this one planet is Vraja-maṇḍala in any universe. So when you look at the planets in the sky at night, you can understand that none of these other planets contain Vraja-maṇḍala.

When the śloka mentions that Vraja-maṇḍala is not difficult to attain in this world, it means that there is no need for interplanetary travel. You can hop on a boat or an airplane or cross the land and somehow or other get to Vraja-bhūmi. Scientists claim to have gone to the moon, but Prabhupāda and many others concurred that the Americans never went to the moon. It is not so easy to go from one planet to another in this world. But because we have been, by chance, on a national transporter, because we have been allowed to take our birth on this planet, attaining Vraja-maṇḍala is not such a difficult thing. Kṛṣṇa goes on to say that this Vraja-maṇḍala is not difficult to attain. And then He also says that Kārtika comes every year. In other words, you don't have to wait lifetimes and lifetimes to get a chance to come to Vraja-maṇḍala during Kārtika. Still, the fools continue to swim in the ocean of repeated birth and death, because they don't come to Vraja-maṇḍala during Kārtika (Mathura-mahatmya, verse 177). All devotional service that you perform when you come to Vṛndāvana-dhāma is multiplied; the benefit is multiplied one thousand times, according to Śrīla Prabhupāda. And also during Kārtika any devotional service is multiplied a thousand times. So in effect, whatever devotional service we are able to perform, if we will do that devotional service in Vraja-maṇḍala during Kārtika, we will get the benefit of a million times the very same devotional service that we would perform any other time in the year, anywhere else in the world.

So to come to Vṛndāvana-dhāma during Kārtika and perform devotional service for the pleasure of Rādhā and Kṛṣṇa, that is the easiest way, or one of the easiest ways, to become kṛta-puṇya-puñjāḥ, to accumulate puṇya in our transcendental bank accounts so that we can play with Kṛṣṇa or hope to play with Kṛṣṇa and dance with Kṛṣṇa as did the cowherd boys and the gopīs:

itthaṁ satāṁ brahma-sukhānubhūtyā
dāsyaṁ gatānāṁ para-daivatena
māyāśritānāṁ nara-dārakeṇa
sākaṁ vijahruḥ kṛta-puṇya-puñjāḥ

In this way, all the cowherd boys used to play with Krsna, who is the source of the Brahman effulgence for jñanis desiring to merge into that effulgence, who is the Supreme Personality of Godhead for devotees who have accepted eternal servitorship, and who for ordinary persons is but another ordinary child. The cowherd boys, having accumulated the results of pious activities for many lives, were able to associate in this way with the Supreme Personality of Godhead. How can one explain their great fortune? SB 10.12.7-11

Now, we should, with an analytical mind, scientifically understand the principles of cause and effect. Why is it that someone seems to be having a greater or a stronger śraddhā than someone else, who is having very pliable or weak śraddhā? Śraddhā means "faith", or regard for devotional service, regard for the beauty of Kṛṣṇa, the sweetness of Kṛṣṇa.

It is mentioned in śāstra that regard is created by an accumulation of sukṛti from previous lifetimes and in this present lifetime.

yeṣāṁ tv anta-gataṁ pāpaṁ
janānāṁ puṇya-karmaṇām
te dvandva-moha-nirmuktā
bhajante māṁ dṛḍha-vratāḥ
(Bhagavad-gītā 7.28)

Do you know this śloka? It says that only in one whose sinful reactions have been completely eradicated and who has accumulated kṛta-puṇya, heaps of piles of pious activities in this life and in previous lives – only in him, who is free from this dualistic mentality, will this preponderant delusion of the dualistic conception of good and bad, favorable and unfavorable, auspiciousness or inauspiciousness, become manifest; bhajante māṁ dṛḍha-vratāḥ, that he can worship Kṛṣṇa with a firm vow, with great determination.

So if we want prema – because premā pumartho mahān, prema is the ultimate goal of our life – if we want prema, we will be concentrating on doing those things that will actually help us to get prema. That will be the mark of our śraddhā.

Bhaktivinoda Ṭhākura mentions in Jaiva Dharma that śraddhā and śaraṇāgati are practically synonymous. If one is claiming to have śraddhā, he also has to have śaraṇāgati. And śaraṇāgati has six characteristics, as mentioned in The Nectar of Devotion.

ānukūlyasya saṅkalpaḥ
prātikūlyasya varjanam
rakṣiṣyatīti viśvāso

goptṛtve varaṇaṁ tathā
ātma-nikṣepa-kārpaṇye
ṣaḍ-vidhā śaraṇāgatiḥ
(Śrī Satvata-tantra: 73)

The first characteristic is to accept only those things that are favorable for the cultivation of uttamā-bhakti. The second characteristic is that one will reject anything that is detrimental to his progress. The third characteristic is to know that Kṛṣṇa is our only protector. The fourth is to be completely dependent on Kṛṣṇa's mercy, which also comes in various ways: Hari, guru, Vaiṣṇava, Bhagavad-gītā. The fifth principle is to not have any separate interest than the interest of Kṛṣṇa. And the sixth principle, last but not least, is to always remain meek and humble.

"Meek and humble" means to have enough su-medhasaḥ, brain substance, to realize that we're patita, low. If we can understand that we are most fallen and that we are practically bereft of much good qualification, then we will understand the importance of taking shelter of the process that Śrī Caitanya Mahāprabhu came to give for the deliverance of the patita – as patita-pāvana, Śrī Caitanya Mahāprabhu, who has given this saṅkīrtana-yajña.

tṛṇād api sunīcena taror iva sahiṣṇunā
amāninā mānadena kīrtanīyaḥ sadā hariḥ
(Śrī Śrī Śikṣāṣṭakam, verse 3)

So, kīrtanīyaḥ sadā hariḥ – performing saṅkīrtana-yajña – is based on this humility. And it is also the medium by which we can accomplish the business of having no interest separate from the interest of Kṛṣṇa, accepting being completely dependent on Kṛṣṇa's mercy, because the saṅkīrtana process is Lord Caitanya's special mercy upon the fallen conditioned souls, and it is the safest place – kīrtana-rasa is the safest place in this material world. Prabhupāda has said like that, that the kīrtana-rasa is the safest place in the material world, indicating that it's the best way to avail oneself to Kṛṣṇa's protection.

Kīrtana-rasa is also the best thing for anartha-nivṛtti. Ceto-darpaṇa-mārjanam means to reject those things that are unfavorable in the cultivation of bhakti, and according to our ācāryas, the congregational chanting of the Holy Names of Kṛṣṇa, nāma-kīrtana or nāma-saṅkīrtana, is the primary, most powerful, and most important aṅga of positive pure devotional service, which is to be accepted for the cultivation of prema via the medium of uttamā-bhakti.

If we want prema, if we can ascertain that this is our actual goal of life and we have no other goal, when your desire is big enough that there are no other desires in your heart, or even if there are any other desires in the heart, then:

akāmaḥ sarva-kāmo vā
mokṣa-kāma udāra-dhīḥ
tīvreṇa bhakti-yogena
yajeta puruṣaṁ param
(Śrīmad-Bhāgavatam 2.3.10)

Even if there are other desires in the heart, then tīvreṇa bhakti-yogena. Bhakti-yoga is characterized by kīrtana. We should engage in saṅkīrtana-yajña and realize the great benefit of doing this saṅkīrtana-yajña in Vṛndāvana-dhāma during Kārtika in order to amass the necessary sukṛti. And to see the benefit of taking bath in Yamunā on days like today, for instance, when it is mentioned in śāstra that the attainment of Goloka-dhāma is easily achieved by doing such a simple thing. We come to Vṛndāvana, and śāstra is telling us that this is a great opportunity, so we should take it! If we have śraddhā, we should take it. And if you don't have śraddhā, you should also take it, in order to get, to increase, your sukṛti so that your śraddhā can become stronger.

I think most of you must have śraddhā – otherwise you would not be here. Still, the śraddhā should be strengthened. There are gradual stages from śraddhā to niṣṭhā. Niṣṭhā means very strong. The mark of your śraddhā will be steadiness in your devotional practice, and that is called niṣṭhā. And niṣṭhā turns into āsakti. Āsakti means intense attachment to the lotus feet of Kṛṣṇa. When that āsakti is there, then Kṛṣṇa's antaraṅga-śakti, His hlādinī-śakti, svarūpa-śakti, may be pleased to bless us with bhāva and prema.

So that was the preliminary class. I'm also a very fallen soul, and on account of that, it's difficult for me to control my tongue. You may know that when Aindra Dāsa speaks, he may say any damned thing – so watch out! But in the way these statements will come out of my mouth, with your intelligence, you might find that it is acceptable from one perspective or another. And another problem is that I have a tendency to talk and talk.

So it usually takes time for me to express myself, because I have a tendency to cover details in order to analyze the subject matters for our benefit. So I told Kṛṣṇa Candra Prabhu [the Russian translator] that if he is not prepared or if you are not prepared to stay with me at least up until ten o'clock, probably even eleven, then perhaps I should not give class. These chapters are so deep and so sweet that we should spend at least a little time with them. These chapters we are studying now in Śrīmad-Bhāgavatam are not for sweeping under the rug. They are not for getting it over, so to speak; they are for relishment. And to be honest with you, I could and I wouldn't mind spending all day long discussing these topics from various angles of vision. Not that I'm so capable, but due to my fallen nature, it takes me considerable time to hash it out. So if you'll bear with me. [Reading from Śrīmad-Bhāgavatam 10.30.11, purport]:

" 'O friend, wife of the deer, from the bliss in your clear eyes we can tell that Śrī Kṛṣṇa has expanded your joy with the beauty of His limbs, His face, and so forth. You are eager to realize the ecstasy of seeing Kṛṣṇa, and thus, your eyes are following Him. In fact, He is never lost to you.'

"Then the gopīs, seeing the doe, continued to walk in their natural way and exclaimed, 'Oh, are you telling us that you have seen Kṛṣṇa? Look, as the deer walks she constantly turns her head back to us as if to say, "I will show Him to you. Just follow me and I will show you Kṛṣṇa." ' " [Śrīmad-Bhāgavatam 10.30.11, purport]

"In this merciless Vṛndāvana" – an interesting thing he is saying here – "In this merciless Vṛndāvana she is the only merciful person." Why? Because Vṛndāvana is not revealing to them the Lord of their hearts – so they're considering Vṛndāvana to be merciless. And only the doe is merciful because she is taking them to Kṛṣṇa. "As the gopīs followed the doe, they happen to lose sight of her and they cry out, 'Oh, why can't we see the deer who is showing us the way to Kṛṣṇa?'

"One gopī suggests that Kṛṣṇa must be somewhere in the vicinity and that the deer, being afraid of Him, must have hidden herself to avoid the possible mistake of revealing His presence."

That means that she is apprehending that Kṛṣṇa is trying to hide Himself and wouldn't be pleased if she would audaciously do anything to reveal His presence or whereabouts. So as to avoid any displeasure in Kṛṣṇa, to avoid His wrath, so to speak, she would prefer not to put herself in such a situation.

This is the last paragraph to the purport: "One gopī suggests that Kṛṣṇa must be somewhere in the vicinity and the deer, being afraid of Him, must have hidden herself to avoid the possible mistake of revealing His presence. Conjecturing in this way, the gopīs detect a fragrance that has by chance blown their way, and they repeatedly declare with great joy, 'Yes, yes, this is it!' "

They are saying that we're on the right track. " 'By Kṛṣṇa's physical contact with His girlfriend, His jasmine garland was smeared with the kuṅkuma powder on Her breasts, and the fragrances of all these things are reaching us.' Thus, the gopīs smelled the aroma of the two lovers' bodies, of Kṛṣṇa's jasmine garland, and of the cosmetic powder [of kuṅkuma] on the breasts of his lover," who happens to be Śrīmatī Rādhārāṇī. Hare Kṛṣṇa. That's the end of the purport.

I want to read you something from another book by Viśvanātha Cakravartī Ṭhākura, called Prema-sampuṭa, which will give a very insightful explanation of Kṛṣṇa's purpose in leaving the gopīs behind, which we were studying in this section. But before I do that, I would just like to make a point – although perhaps not so scholarly, but let's say scientific, on the purpose of bhāgavata-dharma and the absorption in bhāgavata-kathā, as well as the actual goal of Lord Caitanya's saṅkīrtana movement.

Who has not yet read Caitanya-caritāmṛta? It's not yet published in Russian? Anyhow, you may have heard the famous Teachings of Lord Caitanya? That's basically a summary study of Śrī Caitanya-caritāmṛta.

So you must be familiar with the idea that Lord Caitanya came to show the people of Kali-yuga how to become a devotee and what kind of a devotee to become. Although this involves a little discussion on the distinction of Mahāprabhu's internal reason for His advent and His external reason for His advent – there is no time to go into that in depth, but we should understand in gist, that Mahāprabhu's external reason and His internal reason are both integrally related, interdependent, or, you can say, inter-supportive.

When Mahāprabhu desires to relish rādhā-bhāva and also when He desires to relish sakhī-bhāva and mañjarī-bhāva – in all these cases – it should be understood that because Rādhā's bhāva culminates in the experience that She has within Her heart, the ānanda that is within Her heart (and similarly with sakhī-bhāva and mañjarī-bhāva), that experience culminates in the realization of ten million times the happiness of Her own happiness of meeting with Kṛṣṇa by making the arrangement for others to meet with Kṛṣṇa.

Mahāprabhu's internal reason is for relishing rādhā-bhāva. But relishing Rādhā's bhāva also is inclusive of various other things. Please remember that Kṛṣṇa wants to relish rādhā-bhāva. And why does He want to relish rādhā-bhāva? If you read Kṛṣṇa book, you may remember that Kṛṣṇa has told to the gopīs that, "Even if I were to attempt for a lifetime of the demigods or for the lifetime of Brahmā, still I would not be able to repay what I owe you for your completely selfless and self-giving loving service." The gopīs, they might have answered Him that, "In fact, You say that you cannot pay, that it's impossible to repay our service, but we say that 'impossible' is a word in a fool's dictionary!"

I'm not going to say what you want me to say; I'm going to say what I want to say according to my realizations. So I may be including, within this discussion, my own purports as well, but they're not unfounded. And if you simply try to catch the drift of what I'm saying, it may increase or enhance your appreciation of these topics. Someone may argue, "What makes Aindra Dāsa think that he has the right to purport anything?" But I say that at the lotus feet of Śrīla Prabhupāda and for his pleasure and for following in his footsteps, I endeavor to fulfill his instruction that one should speak according to one's realizations. Although I don't claim to have high, high realizations – I'm not so impudent – still I don't see any real need to check the flow of my heart. So I'm going to tell it like it is.

The gopīs will say, or perhaps we can answer, "You say 'impossible', but we say that 'impossible' is a word in the fool's dictionary. We say that there is a way that You can repay Your debt. And how can You repay Your debt? It's that You put Yourself in our shoes and see how it feels."

What they really mean to say, in this regard, is that because we experience ten million times the happiness that You experienced in our loving reciprocation, we want You to experience the happiness that we're experiencing. Otherwise, what is the meaning of You being the supreme enjoyer?" And they're saying, "Don't worry! We will help You to repay Your debt. We're not so hard-hearted as You!"

So how does Kṛṣṇa repay His debt to the gopīs? And gopīs means Rādhārāṇī, Her sakhīs, Her maidservants and not only the gopīs, but all the other devotees of Kṛṣṇa – they also want to see that their services are appreciated.

ekala īśvara kṛṣṇa, āra saba bhṛtya
yāre yaiche nācāya, se taiche kare nṛtya
(Śrī Caitanya-caritāmṛta, Ādi-līlā 5.142)

There is only one iśvara; all others are servants. And every servant wants to feel appreciated. And the best way to appreciate – it's just like if you give me some nice mahā-prasāda, but you didn't taste it and I taste it and I explain how relishable it is, then I want to give you the same mahā-prasāda in order for you to actually understand what it is that you have given me.

One time, Śrīla Prabhupāda argued, "Which is best, which is better – to be honey or to taste honey?" Kṛṣṇa is like honey, but Rādhārāṇī, who is the root of all other varieties of devotees, She is the taster of honey. The taste of tasting honey is ten million times more enchanting than the taste of being honey. In this way, Kṛṣṇa desires to become rasika-śekhara, or the relisher of rasa. In order to fulfill that impossible proposition of repaying the debt, or the impossible proposition of tasting rasa, Rādhārāṇī has joined with Kṛṣṇa in the form of Śrī Caitanya Mahāprabhu in order to facilitate this.

There are two tattvas manifest and acting simultaneously in the body of Caitanya Mahāprabhu, in the person of Mahāprabhu. Internally Mahāprabhu is Kṛṣṇa, and externally He is Rādhā. Externally means the bhāva and the beauty which Kṛṣṇa is relishing is Rādhā. So not only is Kṛṣṇa active within the body of Mahāprabhu, but Rādhā is also active within the body of Mahāprabhu. So in this way, we should understand that not only is Kṛṣṇa desiring to relish Rādhā's bhāva and the bhāvas of various other servants, just like you will see in Caitanya-bhāgavata that Mahāprabhu is relishing many varieties of bhāvas. Sometimes Mahāprabhu is relishing the bhāva of a cowherd boy. This is described also in Navadvīpa-bhāva-taraṅga by Bhaktivinoda Ṭhākura, that He is reciprocating in His midday pastimes with the gopas of Navadvīpa in the mood of Gopāla, Kṛṣṇa Himself. And also, in Caitanya-bhāgavata, you will see that He is relishing Balarāma's bhāva. Balarāma is the Supreme Personality of servitor-Godhead and He loves to serve Kṛṣṇa in varieties of ways.

In order to repay His debt to Balarāma, Mahāprabhu – or Kṛṣṇa in the form of Mahāprabhu – is also relishing His bhāva, or appreciating His standpoint. And also, you will see that Mahāprabhu is relishing Nārāyaṇa-bhāva, Nṛsiṁha's bhāva, Varāha's bhāva, and Rāmacandra's bhāva in relationship with Murāri Gupta particularly – He is exhibiting that mood.

As a matter of fact, Murāri Gupta sees Mahāprabhu as none other than his worshipable Raghunātha. And also, we will see that Mahāprabhu, when He began to display before His associates His desire to relish the varieties of strī-bhāva – strī-bhāva means the feminine aspect of Godhead, He enacted a play in Candraśekhara's house.

In that play you will remember how Śacī-mātā and the others in the audience were totally mystified to understand that Mahāprabhu was playing the role of Rukmiṇī, playing the role of Lakṣmī, even playing the role of goddess Kālī and various others also. He was relishing all these standpoints.

The point of all this discussion here is that gaura-līlā includes His desire to relish Rādhārāṇī's bhāva, and Rādhārāṇī's bhāva is inclusive of the experience that She has in making th arrangements for others to meet with Kṛṣṇa. And not only that, but because Rādhā is active within the body of Mahāprabhu, Rādhā also has a desire to experience the standpoint of Her assistants, Her associates, Her sakhīs, etcetera. So when Mahāprabhu is relishing the mood of Rādhā, that is the fulfillment of Kṛṣṇa's desire to relish Rādhā's bhāva. But when Mahāprabhu is relishing the sakhī-bhāva, the mood of Lalitā-devī or the mood of Rūpa-mañjarī, then this is the fulfillment not only of Kṛṣṇa's desire to relish the standpoint of His different servants, but also of Rādhā's desire to relish the standpoint of Her maidservants. In this way, Rādhārāṇī also fulfills Her desires to repay Her debts to Her sakhīs and maidservants for their kind assistance.

And for that purpose, we can understand that by augmenting saṅkīrtana for the benefit of the fallen conditioned souls, not only Mahāprabhu, not only Mahāprabhu's associates, but according to Śrīla Prabhupāda in

Caitanya-caritāmṛta, anyone can experience ten million times the happiness of their own meeting with Kṛṣṇa by assisting to make arrangements for others to come forward and meet with Kṛṣṇa. Mahāprabhu, in this way, is teaching by His own example how to relish rasa by augmenting or propagation of the saṅkīrtana mission.

In this way, we can understand how attaching oneself to the external activity of propagating saṅkīrtana, which was the external purpose of Mahāprabhu's advent, also facilitates the relishment or the realization of the internal purpose of a devotee in his cultivation of bhajana. There is really no dichotomy involved, because one is serving to facilitate the other.

However, we should understand that this inter-facilitation doesn't happen unless we're simultaneously cultivating the internal bhāva, or the mood. It is very necessary to cultivate the mood of following in the footsteps of the vraja-vāsīs in the cores of our absorption in saṅkīrtana-līlā. Otherwise, it tends to be external; the external form without internal substance or spirit.

Pūrṇacandra Prabhu: It is sometimes said that for realization, where one does one thing and then because of that, he feels he is doing it superficially, then he bounces way over to the other side..., like this?

Aindra Prabhu: If someone is doing it externally and then is realizing that he is lacking heart, lacking the substance, and if the pendulum goes all the way to the other side of neglecting the external program of assisting in the deliverance of other souls to the lotus feet of Kṛṣṇa, then what happens is that he may get something from going internal, but he misses out on the ten million times the happiness that one experiences. He gets one unit of happiness, and that's better than getting nothing if he is parched and not having any mood, any substance, or not feeling that he is getting the substance in relationship to the external service of performing saṅkīrtana.

But really, there's a very simple solution to the problem. Viśvanātha Cakravartī, Ṭhākura in Rāga-vartma-candrikā, makes the point that in the matter of rāga-bhajana, smaraṇa, or līlā-smaraṇa, is essential.

Raga-bhajan has been practiced in many yugas. You may be surprised to know that according to the Padma Purāṇa, Ambarīṣa Mahārāja practiced the cultivation of gopī-bhāva by following the system of aṣṭa-kālīya-līlā-smaraṇa. We're not advocating a gopī-bhāva club now, but because there is such a thing as gopī-bhāva, it's sometimes necessary to say the word gopī-bhāva so that people will understand what we're talking about, or at least have some indication.

You'll also be interested to know that Kṛṣṇa told the mighty warrior Arjuna on the battlefield of Kurukṣetra, sarva-dharmān parityajya (Bhagavad-gītā 18.66). Give up all other religious occupations. That means to give up varṇāśrama-dharma; it means to give up any dharma other than mām ekaṁ śaraṇaṁ vraja – Vraja-dhāma. Vraja means "go," but hidden within that word is the indication as to where to go. He said to give up all other occupations except for this occupation, which will help one to go to Vraja-dhāma. This means to give up attachment to the aiśvarya of Lakṣmī-Nārāyaṇa-pūjā; and it means to give up the attachment to the aiśvarya-bhakti of Dvārakā, aiśvarya-mayī or jñāna-mayī-bhakti of Dvārakā.

All those various dharmas are conditional dharmas. It's not that conditioned souls are only materially conditioned souls; souls can also be spiritually conditioned souls, and as such, he may attach himself to various conditional dharmas. And by doing so, he becomes relegated or confined to a conditional realm.

One conditional realm may be said to be the Devī-dhāma, because there is material conditioning. Another conditional realm may be said to be Vaikuṇṭha, or Maheśa-dhāma. They are conditional realms because the soul's inherent capacity for unconditional love, for unconditional devotion, is not manifest in those realms.

The only unconditional love, kevala-bhakti … because after all, Śrī-guru-caraṇa-padma, kevala-bhakati-sadma – we are supposed to be seeing in our guru that cultivation, or the manifestation of kevala-bhakti, and we expect to get that kevala-bhakti from guru. That kevala-bhakti, that unconditional love, is manifest only in the realm of Vraja, and only by cultivating that unconditional kevala-bhakti is one eligible to enter into that unconditional realm, that realm of unconditional love.

Pūrṇacandra Prabhu: You don't mind me asking questions as we go along?
Aindra Prabhu: Yes, it's okay, sure. As long as we don't forget the spot.

Pūrṇacandra Prabhu: Kevala-bhakti can also be attained in Goloka Navadvīpa, because some devotees are audārya –

Aindra Prabhu: No, no, there is no difference between Vraja and Navadvīpa.

Pūrṇacandra Prabhu: But for some devotees who gravitate towards the audārya instead of mādhurya, they will not be –

Aindra Prabhu: No, that is kevala-bhakti. Yes, Vraja has two compartments: there is the Kṛṣṇa-pīṭha of Vraja, and there is the Gaura-pīṭha of Vraja. Both of them are Vraja; they are both in the realm of Vraja. So kevala-bhakti is certainly found in Nitya-navadvīpa, Gaura-pīṭha.

We were discussing about Arjuna being instructed on the battlefield of Kurukṣetra that māṁ ekaṁ śaraṇaṁ vraja. Sarva-dharmān parityajya, māṁ ekaṁ śaraṇaṁ vraja (Bhagavad-gītā 18.66). This is a little bit of a Bhagavad-gītā class also, because the A, B, C, D's are sometimes required just to get a foundation on what we are talking about in the Bhāgavatam. The Bhagavad-gītā is to set the stage for the cultivation of vraja-bhakti.

In the Pātāla-khaṇḍa of Padma Purāṇa, we read that in fact, Arjuna took that instruction very seriously, and he developed a great curiosity to see the realm of Vraja. He requested Kṛṣṇa to please tell him about that realm of Vraja, where His childhood pastimes took place, and that he heard that there was dancing with gopīs and all these things. And Kṛṣṇa said, "Come on, Arjuna!" Something like that, expressing, "Come on, Arjuna, we are warriors! You don't want to hear about all these things?" That was Kṛṣṇa's mood. He said, "Yes, this is my dhāma. Yes, those are my folks." But then he told Arjuna, "But it is better that you not ask this question."

So Arjuna became very depressed, and he practically became senseless, because Kṛṣṇa was denying him, denying his request. Then Kṛṣṇa, to pacify him, picks him up and embraces him to his heart and tells to Arjuna, "Not only are you going to hear about it, but you are actually going to experience it!" Not only see, but experience! "If you really want to experience, you should go to do this – there was one pīṭha or sitting place where a form of goddess Durgā, Kātyāyanī, was situated. Durgā has many names, but in fact, she was Kātyāyanī-devī, Yogamāyā. And Kṛṣṇa told Arjuna that he should worship her and follow her instructions and then his desire would be fulfilled.

So in short, Kātyāyanī instructed the maidservants, after Arjuna practiced the chanting of certain mantras, to bathe him in the Eastern shore of a particular lake and he had to come out on the Western shore.

When he came out on the Western shore of the lake, he came out as a gopī. The maidservants of Yogamāyā took him to the lake and he bathed in that lake and then he proceeded from the Western side of the lake and was astonished to see that he had been transformed into Arjunīyā Gopī.

So in this way, Arjunīyā Gopī met with all of Rādhārāṇī's sakhīs, and they took her to the feet of Rādhārāṇī, and after worshiping the feet of Rādhārāṇī, when

Kṛṣṇa saw that Arjunīyā Gopī had surrendered herself to Śrīmatī Rādhārāṇī, He took her by the hand and pulled her close to Him and then, with Rādhārāṇī's permission, took her to the nikuñja and sported with her for a long time.

As Arjuna, the great warrior of Mahābhārata, he experienced that as Arjunīyā Gopī his ānanda had increased millions of times. In fact, you will see that Arjunīyā Gopī is actually the original vraja-svarūpa of Arjuna. After Arjuna's desires were fully satisfied to the nth degree, to the topmost limit, Kṛṣṇa instructed one of the sakhīs, one of the maidservants, to take Arjuna, Arjunīyā Gopī, who must have been very tired after so many pleasure pastimes, that she should be relieved of her tiredness by bathing in the Western shore of the lake. So Arjunīyā Gopī bathed in the Western shore of the lake and then popped out on the Eastern shore as Arjuna. When Arjuna realized that he was again Arjuna, instead of Arjunīyā Gopī, he became very, very depressed and distressed, and he fell down in a swoon.

At that time, Vāsudeva Kṛṣṇa came and picked Arjuna up and restored him to his so-called "original" composition or composure as a warrior, a friend of Kṛṣṇa. The only difference was that now, Arjuna was a different Arjuna. Now this Arjuna could always remember, always recall, the sweetness and the transcendental ecstasy within his heart of being Arjunīyā Gopī in the vraja-līlās. In other words, he had established in his heart the vraja-bhāvas. So in this way we should go to Vraja.

We are so fortunate to be in Vraja. We may have to go back to the battlefield, but the question is, Are we going back there with the vraja-bhāvas? The importance is the cultivation of the selfless loving service attitude of the vraja-vāsīs. It's not enough just to plant our body here, although that is also beneficial, because Vṛndāvana is like a desire tree. If you desire bhukti or mukti, Vṛndāvana easily gives it to you. But if you desire kevala-bhakti, unalloyed unconditional loving service spirit, then Vṛndāvana easily grants that, but you have to desire it.

Kṛṣṇa generally doesn't give unalloyed kevala-bhakti very easily. In other tīrthas – I'm giving a synopsis of what is described concerning this topic in the Mathurā-māhātmya – Kṛṣṇa doesn't give vraja-bhakti, or kevala-bhakti, unalloyed devotion, very easily, because He becomes conquered by that love.

In other tīrthas, Kṛṣṇa awards the fruits of karma and jñāna in the form of bhukti and mukti, but in Vraja-dhāma, especially during Kārtika, Kṛṣṇa easily awards unalloyed devotion, especially during these last five days, Bhiṣma-pañcaka – by performing the Bhiṣma-pañcaka fast. Of course, all of you may not be aware of what that is all about. But next year, if you come, or next year if you plan to stay here, you should take advantage of the Bhiṣma-pañcaka fast, because by performing Bhiṣma-pañcaka, it is told that you don't even have to endeavor for unalloyed devotion, but unalloyed devotion comes to your hand. So it is another facility for advancing in Kṛṣṇa consciousness which has been mercifully bestowed upon us by Kṛṣṇa Himself.

This vraja-bhakti, or unalloyed selfless loving service at the lotus feet of Rādhā and Kṛṣṇa, is awarded very easily to the devotee who desires it. That's the key – who desires it. How much do we desire it in Vṛndāvana-dhāma, Vraja-maṇḍala, during the month of Kārtika?

These are important topics of discussion. We should understand that as Mahāprabhu is teaching us how to become devotees, we should never think that Mahāprabhu was advocating anything other than the service of the vraja-vāsīs in the cultivation of vraja-bhakti.

If we are doggedly attached to something else, then Mahāprabhu will allow – so be it! But if we actually want to get the thing which Mahāprabhu came to bestow upon the fallen conditioned souls in this age of Kali, then we should mark this about Mahāprabhu's personality and about Mahāprabhu's mission.

Pūrṇacandra Prabhu: I have another point. About those who don't cultivate something of this mood of selfless service in the mood of the gopīs in Vṛndāvana, and then they realize that they don't have that much going on inside – perhaps they are doing things externally – then, as they don't feel very much, they will have to rush to persons who know some esoteric secrets of vraja-bhajana but who don't cultivate and promote the other side, the preaching of Mahāprabhu's mission, which are many here in Vraja – there are different people like this. So we see that a lot.

Aindra Prabhu: Yeah, but the thing is that an intelligent devotee – hopefully devotees should be a little intelligent – will be able to recognize that Śrīla Prabhupāda is a topmost rasika-vaiṣṇava and that simply by deeply studying Śrīla Prabhupāda's books and following the instructions of Śrīla Prabhupāda in his books, such as to read Bṛhad-bhāgavatāmṛta or to read other gosvāmī literatures, we will get all the necessary inspiration for cultivating the vraja-bhāvas. There is nothing stopping anyone anywhere! It is really not a question of inside ISKCON, or outside ISKCON, or at the feet of this Vaishnava, or at the feet of another Vaishnava. The real question is whether or not we have the intention of intensifying our bhajan. There is nothing stopping anyone from intensifying his bhajan.

Pūrṇacandra Prabhu: But if it's a very important thing that in order to intensify my bhajana, I must go to them –

Aindra Prabhu: No – and maybe not many people are like that, because they are not knowledgeable. They are not having sufficient information to make an intelligent decision – poor fund of knowledge, so therefore they are not able to make an intelligent decision.

I would suggest that in order to come to the proper conclusion, one read this Rāga-vartma-candrikā by Viśvanātha Cakravartī Ṭhākura. In Rāga-vartma-candrikā, there is a point which is very sanguine, very important. Viśvanātha says that although rāga-bhajana does not require reasoning and logic – and say it is based on regard of śāstric injunctions – still, it is absolutely essential to take shelter of the śāstras, because there is no other source of instruction regarding the cultivation of bhāva-bhakti than the śāstras.

The purpose of associating with rasika-vaiṣṇavas is that by associating with them, because they are familiar with the śāstras which appertain to the cultivation of rāga-bhajana, they can point to the conclusions in the śāstras so that you can have easier access to this śāstric information. The same śāstras which have to be consulted in order to get the instructions regarding the cultivation of bhāva-bhakti are there in this mārga or in this Bābājī Mahārāja's maṭha – or ISKCON! The point is that if we are actually serious about bhajana, then deepen your chanting and pursue by scrutinizingly studying the revealed scriptures and associating with devotees who have the inclination toward vraja-bhakti.

Kṛṣṇa Candra Prabhu: In the beginning you said that different devotees have different views of the –

Aindra Prabhu: No, no, no! They all have the same śāstra; there is no other śāstras! It is not that so-and-so Mahārāja in Mathurā and so-and-so bābā at Rādhākuṇḍa, that they are in it themselves, they are having something to produce. They are not having any unique instructions that are not in the śāstras. So consult the śāstras; then you'll get instructions!

Most of the essential śāstras that are dealing with the subject matter of cultivation of rāga-bhajana are translated into English. If they are not translated yet into your language, you can still associate with, via media a translator or whatever, devotees in Śrīla Prabhupāda's movement who are relatively familiar with those śāstras and get considerable guidance.

We didn't get a chance to discuss too much directly about the purport of Śrīmad-Bhāgavatam 10.30.11, and what I want to read you from Viśvanātha Cakravartī Ṭhākura's Prema-samputa deals directly with the subject matter which is very instructive and very important for our understanding of the progress of our devotional life. So, we can take a few short questions.

Kṛṣṇa Candra Prabhu: From many things you said, I got the impression that each soul has his original svarūpa in Vraja, and that means that every personality may attain this goal. This question I have had for a long time, and there are many opinions that different souls have different destinations. Some of them want to be only in Vaikuṇṭha, and others have their destiny in Vraja. So what is your understanding?

Aindra Prabhu: Yes, this is a very good question – fantastic question! So to answer that question is: Yes!

Kṛṣṇa Candra Prabhu.: Each soul has an original form in Vraja?

Aindra Prabhu: Each soul has a particular destiny, destination point. We touched on this when we discussed the principle of materially conditioned souls and spiritually conditioned souls. This is the point – there is a saying that man is the architect of his own destiny. In Bhaktivinoda Ṭhākura's Sri-Kṛṣṇa-saṁhitā, he explains this – that every living entity, every jīva, has the inherent capacity to augment the vraja-bhāvas. Every living entity! However, you will find in Caitanya-caritāmṛta that sometimes we have to put two and two together to come to a conclusion. It is not wrong to do like that, to put two and two together to come to a conclusion. But it will be dependent on your spiritual intelligence, your degree of spiritual intelligence, which depends on your purity as to whether you come to the right conclusion by putting two and two together according to śāstra. Perhaps neophytes should not try to do that too much. But it is not wrong for an advancing devotee to draw conclusions from the śāstras.

Prabhupāda has instructed that there is a difference between mental speculation and philosophical speculation. Mental speculation is coming from the platform of saṅkalpa-vikalpa, on the mental platform, accepting and rejecting things on the basis of what is gratifying to my senses or to my mind. And philosophical speculation means to take the information, which is bona-fide information coming in śāstras, and put two and two together and draw a conclusion from the information at our disposal. In such philosophical speculation, there is always a need to be open for new information, because without being broad-minded, it will not be possible to avail ourselves to spiritual growth. Of the two, mental speculation is blameworthy, whereas philosophical speculation is acceptable.

Pūrṇacandra Prabhu: Mahāprabhu told to Anupama and Murāri Gupta, mām ekaṁ śaraṇaṁ vraja – also one should worship Me in Vraja. But they couldn't, because they were attracted to Rāmacandra. So what about them?

Aindra Prabhu: They are not jīvas.
Pūrṇacandra Prabhu: They are nitya-siddhas.
Aindra Prabhu: It's just like Lakṣmī-devī. That is just like asking, "Why was Lakṣmī-devī unable to attain the rāsa dance with Kṛṣṇa even after so many austerities?" The answer is that they are manifestations of Kṛṣṇa's svarūpa-śakti, which are expanded for a particular purpose only and only are endowed with a particular capacity for reciprocation with the particular Lord of their lives. They are not jīvas. So they are created for their function – or expanded actually, expanded for their particular function.

Before I answer another question, I want to put the two together. There are two in Kṛṣṇa-saṁhitā, and there are another two which I put together with that two in order to complete the equation. Did you reiterate it that Kṛṣṇa-saṁhitā is telling that every living entity, every jīva, has the inherent capacity for augmenting the vraja-bhāvas? That is the one statement.

And also the other two, which we are putting together with those two in order to come up with the conclusion, is that Kavirāja Gosvāmī warns in Caitanya-caritāmṛta that one should be careful not to allow oneself to become attached to the opulence of Lakṣmī-Nārāyaṇa-pūjā, because it will prove to be a stumbling block on the path of progressive vraja-bhakti.

That indicates that if someone allows himself to become attached to something of a lower order, he will not be able to get the higher realization. As far as the cultivation of rāga-bhajana is concerned in the matter of augmenting the vraja-bhāvas within our own heart, Viśvanātha Chakravati Thakur also reveals to us in Rāga-vartma-candrikā that there are five elements which are favorable, unfavorable, or neither favorable or unfavorable in the matter of the cultivation of the vraja-bhāvas, which every living entity can do.

So these elements pertain to both: the stage of perfection and the stage of cultivation. The first element is described as nija-abhīṣṭa-bhāva-maya. This bhāva-maya means to be completely absorbed in one's desired devotional sentiments. That is manifest in the stage of perfection as sthāyi-bhāva. Sthāyi-bhāva means the constant devotional disposition of a soul in one of the five primary rasas.

It also pertains to the sādhaka in that the sādhaka, or the practitioner, will be absorbed – his absorption in the pursuit of that bhāva with the aim of attaining perfection by following in the footsteps of someone who already has mastered the path such as Raktaka, Patraka, or Subala, Śrīdāmā, Nanda – Yaśodā, Rādhā, Lalitā ... So that is bhāva-maya.

Then there is nija-abhīṣṭa-bhāva-sambandhi. This bhāva-sambandhi means those things which connect you with that bhāva or those things which help to bring about the bhāva-maya or the absorption in the pursuit of that bhāva or the absorption in the sthāyi-bhāva itself. This is described as the activities of hearing about Kṛṣṇa, chanting the Holy Names of Kṛṣṇa, performing harināma-saṅkīrtana, bhāgavata-kathā, and other spiritual activities which direct the consciousness toward the desired objective of vraja-bhakti, vraja-prema.

The next section is called nija-abhīṣṭa-bhāva-ānukūla. Have you heard of ānukūlyasya saṅkalpaḥ prātikūlyasya varjanam? Ānukūla means that it is favorable. It is not pratikūla, or unfavorable, but rather favorable. These things are described, such as wearing of the Vaiṣṇava tilaka, or keeping the tulasī-kaṇṭhi-mālā, because these are purifying to the body and the heart and the soul and also help us remember that we are devotees, we are trying to be devotees. And also, the fact that tulasī is so intimately related with Kṛṣṇa. Chanting on the tulasī-mālā is very beneficial.

As a side-point, it may be pointed out that as far as augmenting our chanting of the Holy Name and increasing our adhikāra, our eligibility in the matter of chanting the Holy Name, it's better to be lazy intelligent than active intelligent. You can chant hundreds and hundreds of mālās anywhere in the world, but you get a thousand times the benefit here in Vṛndāvana. You get a million times the benefit by chanting in Kārtika in Vṛndāvana, and if you will chant on mṛdaṅga-shaped beads – you see these mṛdaṅga-shaped beads? They are not round or square, but they are mṛdaṅga-shaped beads. In śāstra, it is told that by chanting on these mṛdaṅga-shaped beads, you get the benefit of chanting one hundred rounds with every round that you chant. So that's one hundred million rounds during Kārtika with every round that you chant. You get one hundred million rounds worth of transcendental credit in your spiritual bank account, which makes it easier for you to come to the platform of dancing with Kṛṣṇa, playing with Kṛṣṇa as the cowherd boys and the gopīs.

When I went out one day on book distribution – because I know book distribution from way back. Most people see me as a harināma-saṅkīrtana fanatic these days, but I spent at least eight years distributing Prabhupāda's books daily. Anyway, one day when I was on book distribution, I again had to go to the bathroom. Damned bathroom! Anyway, my beads – everyone knows the instruction you're not supposed to take your bead bag into the bathroom, right? I learned a great lesson that day, because I was too rigidly following that instruction without really understanding the purpose of the instruction. What is the use of following an instruction if the thing is a disaster in the end?

What I did was that I carefully wrapped my bead bag up – that was at the Kennedy Center in Washington D.C., you know, this huge auditorium? Big performances are put on there, so it was a great opportunity to distribute Prabhupāda's books. So, I wrapped my bead bag up, and I went into a phone booth and pulled out the phone book and put the beads behind the phone book and pushed the phone book back in. And then I went into the bathroom – I was very quick. Within a minute, or a couple of minutes, I did my business and got out and came back and pulled out the phone book. And my beads were gone!

So I lost my beads that were chanted on by Śrīla Prabhupāda. Some devotees may be attached to their beads because they were chanted on by their spiritual master, or whatever, but fortunately or unfortunately, whatever it is... Prabhupāda said that the mark of a Vaiṣṇava is that he knows how to turn a disadvantage into an advantage. So I turned it into an advantage, after I read this passage where it describes that by chanting on mṛdaṅga beads you get a hundred times the benefit. Because my previous beads, chanted on by Prabhupāda, were not mṛdaṅga beads. But anyway, to compensate for the loss, I'm chanting on mṛdaṅga beads and getting a hundred times the benefit of my chanting. Find out!

Another thing is that if you will put tulasī dirt from the tulasī plant on your head or on your body at the time of worship or at the time of chanting, you get the benefit of a hundred days worship or a hundred days chanting of your mālā.

The point is that if you say that you want to advance in Kṛṣṇa consciousness, there are so many simple things you can do. Who can't reach their finger down and take a little mud from a tulasī plant in any ISKCON temple anywhere in the world and put the tulasī dirt on your head? Like the pūjārīs – they have to light a ghee lamp anyway, because they are worshiping the Deity. So they light a ghee lamp. But it says that if you light the ghee lamp with the stick of a dry tulasī plant – if you light the stick and light the ghee lamp – you get the benefit of offering ten million ghee lamps with every ghee lamp that you offer.

So it's such a simple thing! Who will do it? No one is stopping anyone from doing it. If you want to advance in devotional service – of course, you have to know about all these things, but when they are revealed to you, you should immediately catch it up and take advantage of the opportunity to make leaps and bounds of spiritual progress so that you can quickly come to the perfectional stage in this lifetime. It is not going to happen automatically. By the mercy of Kṛṣṇa and by the mercy of Vaiṣṇavas, we may come in contact with various programs or processes or facilities for advancing in devotional service, but it is up to us to take advantage of these things. And then we can make very rapid progress in devotional service, which will make it possible for us to go back home, back to Godhead, in one lifetime. It is not going to be possible by sitting on our butts and doing nothing, being too lazy to put a little tulasī dirt on our heads!

Remember to only burn dry tulasī! Never use the stick of a live tulasī! And it says furthermore in the Tulasī-māhātmya regarding that point (this is Lord Śiva, Sadāṣiva, instructing Nārada Muni) that there is no one more dear to Kṛṣṇa than one who offers a ghee lamp which is lit by the tulasī stick. It's easy to get these sticks while you are in Vṛndāvana, because there is so many tulasīs. At the gośālā, there are probably a great number of dead tulasī trees. So you can go and collect the sticks and have a little can of sticks that lasts you all year until you come the next time. The point is that we want to become dear to Kṛṣṇa!

If śāstra says that there is no one more dear than one who offers a ghee lamp which is lit by the tulasī stick, then do it! Don't waste your valuable human form of life.

Anyway, these are bhāva-ānukūlas. This is a discussion on bhāva-ānukūla. Then there is what is called bhāva-aviruddha. Viruddha means "which is against," and aviruddha means that it is not against.It is not favorable, it's not obstructing, but it's also not connecting you with the bhāva-maya.

So these things are described as... can you guess? Respecting the cow – they are not favorable, but they are not unfavorable. So it is not wrong to do. It is not something which will impede your progress. Respecting the cow, respecting the aśvattha tree or the pippala tree and even respecting brāhmaṇas. It is neither for nor against. Those are the examples that are given.

Then comes nija-abhīṣṭa-bhāva-viruddha, which is against the cultivation of the bhāva. That is in the matter of cultivating rāga-bhajana or vraja-bhakti. If in my heart of hearts, after having read Kṛṣṇa book and seen the beauty of the vraja-līlās being so enchanting, it inspires me with the hope to – at long last, after all my anarthas are set and done – somehow or other go there and be with that flute-playing Kṛṣṇa, the friend of Subala, the lover of Rādhārāṇī, the son of Nanda-Yaśodā. To be with Him, to serve Him in the land of Vraja – if that is awakening in your heart, then you should be very careful to understand what is favorable and what is unfavorable in the matter of actually attaining the desired goal.

The discussion that Viśvanātha Chakravarti Thakur enters into in relationship to nija-abhīṣṭa-bhāva-viruddha – those things which are against the cultivation of the desired bhāva, they are specifically in relationship to certain aspects of vaidhī-bhakti, or let's say they include that. Also the cultivation of karma, what to speak of vikarma. Vikarma – that wasn't mentioned. Karma and jñāna – karma includes both sukarma and vikarma, so that means sinful activities and pious activities. The cultivation of karma and jñāna and also employing various mudrās in the matter of ritualistic performance of Deity worship...

Kṛṣṇa Candra Prabhu: That is against, the mudrās?

Aindra Prabhu: Yes, that is against. Different mudrās are included. You can read it yourself to understand. The cultivation of karma and jñāna – these are things which work against the cultivation of the bhāva. And the use of various types of mudrās that they use in their ritualistic performance of Deity worship – worshiping the Deity in awe and reference, reverential devotion – certain aspects of reverential devotion or devotion in the mood of worshiping Lakṣmī-Nārāyaṇa, which are against the cultivation of the internal vraja-bhāva.

It doesn't mean that in the worship of the Deity in the temple there shouldn't be proper decency and decorum. There should be proper etiquette. There should not be dishonor. And there should not be any vile activity. There should not be any vulgarity, vulgar words, in the Deity worship. Especially for the sādhakas, we have no right to just barge into the affairs of Rādhā and Kṛṣṇa! The Deities are having Their līlā, and we have no right to just inconvenience Them in any way.

Also included in this bhāva-viruddha are the activities of worship of Rukmiṇī-Dvārakādīśa and as well the cultivation of the mood of mahiṣī-bhāva, or following in the footsteps of the queens of Dvārakā in svakīya-rasa. These things are described as being against the cultivation of the moods of Vraja.

Now, we have made this point that there is favorable or unfavorable. If someone attaches himself to the opulence of Lakṣmī-Nārāyaṇa-pūjā or any of these other things which are considered to be as bhāva-aviruddha, then that attachment is a kind of spiritual conditioning which relegates the soul to an inferior realm, because the superior realm does not accommodate those conditional attachments.

It's a question of simply opening our eyes. Jīv jāgo, jīv jāgo – opening your ears, opening your eyes, opening your heart. If our eyes are a little open by the grace of Kṛṣṇa, then we will realize why we have any interest in discussing any such affairs, any subject matters like this. It is because in previous lifetimes, and also in this lifetime, we have come in contact with agents of vraja-bhakti. To the extent that we have served, either knowingly or unknowingly, an agent of vraja-bhakti, to that extent we accumulate jñāta or ajñāta-sukṛti in our transcendental bank account. It is that accumulation of what is called bhakti-unmukhi-sukṛti which strengthens our śraddhā, or faith. If we have not had opportunity to serve the agents of Vraja, and have instead associated with agents of vaikuṇṭha-bhakti, then we will develop the type of śraddhā which is directed toward reverential devotion. It is by associating with the reverential devotees of Godhead that we get the śāstra-visvaśa-mayī-śraddhā which is called as vaidhī-śraddhā.

This is vaidhī-śraddhā, that stage in the reverential process of devotional service as a god-fearing man. This vaidhī-śraddhā is based on reverence and fear and a regard for śāstric injunctions. If someone has had the opportunity to associate with an agent of vraja-bhakti, in this life or in past lives – if not in past lives, at least in this life – he or she is very fortunate. And who can say that they are not associating with Śrīla Prabhupāda? Who can say that they haven't had an opportunity to associate with and serve Śrīla Prabhupāda in his vāṇī manifestion, in the form of his books, in the form of the movement, in the form of his saṅkīrtana mission?

Once a devotee asked Śrīla Prabhupāda, "Which vraja-vāsī should we follow in the footsteps of in order to realize the perfection of vraja-bhakti?" And Prabhupāda said, "I am that vraja-vāsī!" So he directly admitted that "I am that vraja-vāsī!" He is a vraja-vāsī, and by following in his footsteps, by serving him or by having served him, to whatever degree we have actually done the work of surrender, to that degree we can understand, or expect, that this lobha-mayī-śraddhā will gradually be manifesting within our hearts.

Lobha-mayī-śraddhā means sraddhā which is based on a greed to catch up the moods of a vraja-vāsī, to have the greed to follow in the footsteps of a vraja-vāsī. Prabhupāda is that vraja-vāsī. So let's philosophically speculate one more time and put two and two together.

Putting two and two together means that we go back to the beginning of our class about the external and internal purposes in Caitanya Mahāprabhu's appearance, or as devotees following Caitanya Mahāprabhu, our external activities of preaching Kṛṣṇa consciousness and the internal practices of cultivation of vraja-bhakti-bhajana.

So, this is the mood of the vraja-vāsīs that we see in Śrīla Prabhupāda, how he synthesized simultaneously the cultivation of the internal bhajana in relationship to the external cultivation of bhajana in the form of kīrtana for the benefit of others. Both, the internal cultivation and the external propagation of Kṛṣṇa consciousness are integral essentials in our cultivation of vraja-bhakti, or kevala-bhakti, at the feet of our param-kevala-bhakta, Śrīla Prabhupāda. Śrīla Prabhupāda ki jaya!

November 29, 2001

The day after tomorrow is the beginning of the Mārgaśīrṣa month. That is the pratipadā, and that is the beginning of Kātyāyanī-vrata. During this month, the vraja-kumārīs, the young unmarried gopīs, kanyakās, they perform the Kātyāyanī-vrata in order to get Kṛṣṇa as their husband. These were very young girls, only four or five years old.

You can see how it's getting very chilly. In the morning before sunrise, they would rise up and go to Yamunā and take bath just before the sunrise. Just on this Dvādaśī, I took bath in Yamunā and I realized how cold the Yamunā was, even in the middle of the day. So what to speak of how cold it is before this sandhi-prakāśa time when the sun is just rising. At least to some extent, we can appreciate the atmospheric conditions in which the gopīs had performed their austerities to please Kātyāyanī. Just like this – as we were speaking yesterday about how everything should remind us of Kṛṣṇa. So similarly, this cold air in Vṛndāvana is not ordinary cold air, but it is spiritual cold air. It is helping to increase the devotees' determination to express their desires for prema.

Śrīla Prabhupāda said that all the water in Vṛndāvana is liquid prema. Sometimes in the wintertime that liquid prema is very cold, and sometimes in the summertime it's very hot. And sometimes you will experience that the water is salty. Why is the water very salty? It is understood by the local vraja-vāsīs that the water is salty is because when Akrūra took Kṛṣṇa away from the gopīs and away from the vraja-vāsīs, but particularly the gopīs, and took Him to Mathurā for killing Kaṁsa, the gopīs became so overwhelmed with feelings of separation that they shed unlimited tears, which muddied the ground and created pools of salty water, salty tears. The salty tears soaked into the ground and created a salt bed and as the water is coming on the Yamunā water table, it is collecting the salt from the gopīs' tears and that is why the water – much of the water here in Vṛndāvana – is salty.

When we sometimes taste some water and "Oh, it's too salty!", we can think within our mind – it's not wrong to think like this – that Kṛṣṇa is the pure taste of water. But this water is actually devoid of its pure taste, which is symptomatic of the experience of separation from Kṛṣṇa. If we taste this salty water, then we should understand that we're getting a taste of the gopīs' separation from Kṛṣṇa. And when we bathe in this water, we should not regret. Actually, it is the highest goal of the followers of Śrī Caitanya Mahāprabhu, particularly those who are following in the line of Rūpa and Raghunātha – it is the highest goal of the followers of Bhaktisiddhānta Sarasvatī Ṭhākura; it is the highest goal of the followers of Śrīla Prabhupāda – to serve Śrīmatī Rādhārāṇī and the gopīs in their feelings of separation at the time when Akrūra takes Kṛṣṇa from Vṛndāvana.

When we bathe in this salty water – sometimes we have to bathe, and like in the gurukula, there is nothing but salty water, so we're bathing in salty water. Every time we bathe in salty water, we should be conscious of the fact and actually think and meditate on how it is that Vṛndāvana is so merciful, that in so many ways Vṛndāvana is facilitating our advancement in Kṛṣṇa consciousness. Particularly in this situation, Vṛndāvana will be facilitating our bathing in the remnants of the gopīs' vipralambha-prema.

And sometimes we can think that when the water is very cold, these are like cold tears – perhaps not salty tears, but cold tears. And when the water is very hot, they are like hot tears. In other words, we should not see this Vṛndāvana, this land of Vṛndāvana, or anything related to the land of Vṛndāvana, as something mundane or material. This is not an ordinary land. This is non-different from Goloka-dhāma, Vraja-dhāma. Prabhupāda has told that the sky above Vṛndāvana is not the material sky but the spiritual sky. So when we see the stars or the planets or the sun, we should understand that this is actually not the sun of this material world, nor are these the planets of this material world, but rather all the stars in the sky – although in this universe, it is reflected as the milky way or galaxies or any such things, but in reality, these are the arrangements of the Vaikuṇṭhalokas, which are on the outside of the Goloka planet. In Goloka they will stand on the land of Goloka, and they will see the stars in the sky at night. Those stars are Vaikuṇṭhalokas that they are seeing in the spiritual sky.

In this way, we can feel ourselves to be residents of the land of Vraja and always be absorbed in the thoughts of the gopīs' and the vraja-vāsīs' bhāvas, at least admiring those bhāvas to the best of our abilities, and gradually imbibing the actual spirit of what it means to be a vraja-vāsī. After all, we are praying every morning, kṛpā kori' koro tāre vṛndāvana-vāsi. Every devotee in this movement has been given the right to pray to become a vraja-vāsī. Vraja-bhūmi and Goloka-vraja, Goloka-vraja-dhāma, they are identical with each other in practically every respect. The only thing is that in this world there is some contact with the external energy. Sometimes the līlās of this realm of Vraja-bhūmi take a slightly different shape than the līlās of Kṛṣṇa and the vraja-vāsīs in Goloka-dhāma. But in any case, or in either case, we should know that it is far better than going to Vaikuṇṭhaloka is to see the Vaikuṇṭhalokas in the sky from the standpoint of a vraja-vāsī, a resident of Vraja-dhāma.

There are so many ways to expand our absorption in Kṛṣṇa consciousness, both as sādhakas and, more so, as siddha-bhaktas, when we come to that position. Don't waste time! Although we are eternal living entities and will eternally have opportunities for advancing in Kṛṣṇa consciousness, still this human form of life is very rare and there is no guarantee when we will have the opportunity to take the human form of life again. So we should take every opportunity of every waking moment to cultivate our internal as well as external absorption in Kṛṣṇa consciousness.

There are two types of devotees. One is called bhajanānandī, and the other is called goṣṭhyānandī. Śrīla Bhaktisiddhānta Sarasvatī Ṭhākura has stated that the best goṣṭhyānandī is the bhajanānandī who preaches. Prabhupāda and Bhaktisiddhānta, they always try to push us in the direction of becoming goṣṭhyānandī. However, without doing the internal cultivation, or the internal bhajana of deepening one's experiences in Kṛṣṇa consciousness as per the development of our eternal loving sentiments toward Kṛṣṇa in terms of one of the five primary rasas, we can hardly have much to share with others in the matter of the goṣṭhyānandī principle. In this way, the best goṣṭhyānandī is the bhajanānandī who preaches.

I am going to tell you something that may sound a little revolutionary. Śrīla Prabhupāda – about three years ago – appeared to me in a dream. And he told me something that was very profound to me and which helped solidify the direction in my spiritual life. Actually, many years ago, about eighteen years ago, Prabhupāda appeared in a dream also.

I should tell what he said to me in this dream first. As I have told you before, I had spent at least eight years cultivating the vanity of being one of Śrīla Prabhupāda's transcendental book distributors. I remember when I was traveling with the Rādhā-Dāmodara saṅkīrtana party in America, Śrīla Prabhupāda wrote us a letter telling us how his heart went out with the boys who are going out in the vans, distributing books all over the American countryside. Prabhupāda was, as he said, practically whipping us to double and re-double book distribution. Receiving such a letter from Śrīla Prabhupāda was a great inspiration in the matter of increasing our missionary spirit. We should never lose that missionary spirit. At the same time, we should understand that there is some very important work to be done in order to actually be qualified to fulfill our mission.

After Śrīla Prabhupāda left us, I noticed that all over our Society there was a great decline and neglect of the primary process given to us by Lord Caitanya Mahāprabhu in the matter of the congregational chanting of the Holy Names. In Śrīla Prabhupāda's time, we used to go out for fourteen-hour saṅkīrtana days.

We received another letter from Śrīla Prabhupāda in my early Kṛṣṇa consciousness. He wrote to us in Washington D.C., where I was stationed, that he was very, very pleased with our fourteen-hour saṅkīrtana days. We were going out on the streets with dhotī and shaved head and tilaka and chanting and dancing in the public saṅkīrtana party and distributing Back to Godhead magazines side by side with a newsletter, called the Saṅkīrtana Newsletter.

We would weekly report the book-distribution results to Śrīla Prabhupāda. After having received the nineteenth newsletter, Śrīla Prabhupāda wrote to Śrutideva Prabhu. Śrutideva and I had a very friendly relationship, and he called me into the saṅkīrtana office. Actually, it was the book-distribution office, but we were calling it the saṅkīrtana office, and Śrutideva was calling the newsletter the Saṅkīrtana Newsletter. Actually, it was the book-distribution newsletter. Although book distribution is bṛhad-kīrtana, it is called, or considered, by Śrīla Prabhupāda Bhaktisiddhānta Ṭhākura as bṛhad-kīrtana, still Śrīla Prabhupāda made a distinction between saṅkīrtana, the congregational chanting of the Holy Names, and book distribution.

Śrīla Prabhupāda wrote, "I have received your saṅkīrtana newsletter # 19 and I am very pleased to" – I am paraphrasing maybe a little – "I am very pleased to hear about the results of your saṅkīrtana AND book distribution."

This was remarkable! Śrutideva was telling me, "Aindra Prabhu, look at this, look at this!" He was saying that Prabhupāda is making a clear distinction between saṅkīrtana and book distribution here. Because it's the Saṅkīrtana Newsletter, and he was trying to instruct Śrutideva, "I am very pleased to hear the results of your saṅkīrtana AND book distribution."

Then Prabhupāda says, "Actually, this Kṛṣṇa consciousness movement is based on saṅkīrtana, the congregational chanting of the names of Kṛṣṇa." He said, "I started this movement by sitting under a tree at Thompson Square Park and performing saṅkīrtana, or the congregational chanting of the Holy Names of Kṛṣṇa." And then he ended the letter by saying, "Therefore, I want that this saṅkīrtana and book distribution go on side by side."

In our enthusiasm to double and re-double book distribution, we basically pulled our energies out of the saṅkīrtana field and applied them to the book-distribution field – with all good intentions, no doubt. In our religious fervor, we tended to neglect saṅkīrtana, and then when Śrīla Prabhupāda left us all of a sudden, in the middle of all that religious fervor to double and re-double book distribution, there was much confusion created, and we never actually got re-focused on the principle of saṅkīrtana and book distribution being performed side by side.

When a great ācārya leaves, much confusion arises naturally, because different devotees are on different levels. Different devotees are on different platforms of dependency or non-dependency on the vapu-sevā, or the physical presence of the spiritual master. Prabhupāda has told that those who are more neophyte, they depend more one the vapu than on the vani. So when the spiritual master leaves, those who are neophytes, which means those who have a less solidified faith in the Holy Names of Kṛṣṇa or faith in the spiritual import of the instructions of the spiritual master depend more on the vapu than on the vāṇī. After Prabhupāda left, those who were neophytes became confused, and they started to materially calculate as to how to spread the Kṛṣṇa consciousness movement in various ways.

I don't want to get too much into the bleak history, but unfortunately, during those years what became termed "sticker saṅkīrtana" crept into the scene, together with "Korean painting saṅkīrtana" and "carved-candle saṅkīrtana" and "record saṅkīrtana" and even "sex, drugs, and rock-'n'-roll-karmī-record saṅkīrtana." So at any rate, personally I saw a great need to try to push forward the direct performance of harinama-sankirtana. Everyone at that time was going out in karmī clothes, and on the plea of giving people a chance to do some sevā and get some ajñāta-sukṛti, we would approach them and cheat them in various ways, the greatest cheating being that we were not actually surrendered to the principle of yāre dekha, tāre kaha 'kṛṣṇa'-upadeśa āmāra ājñāya guru hañā tāra' ei deśa. (Śrī Caitanya-caritāmṛta, Madhya-līlā 7.128)

We were not telling them about Kṛṣṇa. We wouldn't allow ourselves to even say the words "Hare Kṛṣṇa," because we didn't want to implicate the movement in the infamy that would come about on account of the magnitude of our cheating tactics.

It's not wrong to cheat for Kṛṣṇa, but you have to know how to cheat for Kṛṣṇa, you have to know when to cheat for Kṛṣṇa, you have to know where to cheat for Kṛṣṇa and why to cheat for Kṛṣṇa. It is not wrong to beg, borrow, or steal even for Kṛṣṇa.

Unfortunately, when neophytes try to do these things, much of the time they lose sight of the purpose and they lose sight of the principles and the principle aspects of devotional service. Sometimes they become so divorced from the direct processes of devotional service in their attempt to cheat for Kṛṣṇa that their actual enthusiasm and faith begin to wane, or dwindle.

We saw that book distribution practically came to a standstill all over the world, except maybe for Russia. We saw that, practically speaking, on account of the dwindling of their faith in the Holy Name, the faith in the instructions of the spiritual master became weak. Śrīla Prabhupāda instructed that the finances of the temples, the overhead of the temples' expenses, could be met by the profits from book distribution, and that if there was any problem in that, it could be subsidized by prasādam distribution, not by distributing karmī records and these things that we were doing. Because of doing things which were outside the principles of the instructions of the spiritual master, it covered our intelligence considerably. At least the intelligence of the neophyte devotees became considerably covered and they began to lose faith in the instructions of the spiritual master on account of their not actually applying the instructions and gaining the realizations of the duty and the efficacy or the power of those instructions.

Because of all that, it was seen that practically all over the world, book distribution came to a halt. I saw it was practically impossible to get anyone to go on book distribution; hardly anyone was going out. There were a few determined stalwarts going out, but not like it was in previous years when Śrīla Prabhupāda was here, and probably only 10 percent of what was happening when Prabhupāda was here. Also, I noticed that in a temple where I had experienced more than 250 devotees going out having tumultuous kīrtana every weekend for mahā-saṅkīrtana, in that same temple after Śrīla Prabhupāda left it was like pulling teeth – how hard it was to pull teeth to get even 8 or 9 devotees to go on the mahā-harināma-saṅkīrtana at a temple of about 120 who were there at that time.

Needless to say, in my heart of hearts, I saw a need to at least try to push back in the other direction by trying to, in my small little way, augment a consciousness of the need to perform harināma-saṅkīrtana in our Society.

My practical experience as a book distributor was that it was the harināma-saṅkīrtana which gave life to my book distribution. I was also a pujari, I was having double duties. I would do the pūjā and dressing the Deities in the morning, and then I would go out all day on book distribution. So I practically experienced that it was harināma-saṅkīrtana which gave life to my Deity worship.

If I was ever into trying to cook for the Deities in the kitchen, it was the harināma-saṅkīrtana which drifted into the service of cooking for the Deities in the kitchen; it was harināma-saṅkīrtana that was the life of my cooking. And if I was ever asked to go to clean the toilets, my practical experience was that it was the harināma-saṅkīrtana which was sustaining me.

Due to my practical experience of the effectiveness of harināma-saṅkīrtana increasing my individual Kṛṣṇa consciousness and seeing how, when we were doing harināma-saṅkīrtana, the Kṛṣṇa consciousness of the collective community was also considerably greater than at that time, the present time when I was seeing the decline and all of this after Prabhupāda's disappearance, because I saw these things and I practically experienced these things, I felt that at least somebody – not that I have any power to anything really – but that somebody should make an attempt to bring it to everybody's attention that we should focus more on the direct principal process of harināma-saṅkīrtana.

So I decided that I should create a harināma-saṅkīrtana festival program in New York, and in order to do that nicely with nice stage props, I came to India to collect some nice decorative cloth from Pipili, a city outside of Jagannātha Purī, for making umbrellas and different paraphernalia for my festival program. When I was arranging for shipping that paraphernalia back to America, I contacted one of our life members, who happened to be in charge of the cargo section of the international airport in Delhi.

I'm not discussing this just to tell my life history, but remember, this is in relationship to a dream which appeared to me – two dreams. There is a purpose behind my wanting to tell you these dreams. Excuse my complex psyche!

So this manager of the cargo section of the airport begged me to come to his home. He had taken birth in the brāhmaṇa community, but when I reached his home, I saw that there was a little Western poodle dog running in and out of his house, having free run of the house. I immediately ascertained that this man could hardly be following very strictly the brahminical principles. Since he was a Bengali, I thought, "Well, maybe he is eating fish." Usually if there is a dog around, there is some meat-eating involved. When they offered me prasāda, I refused to accept anything other than uncut fruits. And that was also at great risk.

Acyutānanda – bless his heart – told me that Śrīla Prabhupāda had instructed him in relationship to his life membership program here in India, that unless a life member or someone whom we are preaching to become a life member is following the four regulative principles and chanting a minimum of sixteen rounds, we should be careful not even to accept an offering of water from that person. Since this man invited me and I was to stay the night with him in order to do the work early the next morning, I felt like I was put in an awkward position, because in India, the customs are a little bit different perhaps than in some places like the West, because if you don't eat, they feel offended. If you don't accept something from their hand, they may feel offended.

Since he was offering to help me get the job done for cheaper, because I was low in funds and I was alone and I didn't have financial backing at that time, I was thinking as not to offend him. So I dared to accept some whole fruit from him, because at least the whole fruit wouldn't be cut by knifes that might have been used for cutting meat. This was the first night in my whole Kṛṣṇa conscious career that I spent the night on another man's turf, although he was a life member.

That evening when I took rest, Śrīla Prabhupāda appeared to me in a dream. This was the first dream. When Prabhupāda appeared in my dream – of course, I don't know how many of you have ever experienced Prabhupāda appearing in your dreams, but when he appears in his dreams, it's a supra-phenomenal experience, means it is a supra-mundane experience, it is completely spiritual and having transcendental profundity.

Śrīla Prabhupāda asked me in the dream, "Aindra, what are you doing?" And then I began to enthusiastically explain to him how I was collecting things to make a nice harināma-saṅkīrtana festival for him in New York City. Then, just because of the presence of Śrīla Prabhupāda and the circumstances, it suddenly hit me that I had given up the vanity of being one of Śrīla Prabhupāda's transcendental book distributors.

And due to Śrīla Prabhupāda's presence, this realization that I had given up the vanity hit me very hard in the dream, and suddenly I began pouring incessant tears from my eyes, and I told Śrīla Prabhupāda that I was sorry that I had given up book distribution [beginning to cry]. I was always impressed that this is our number-one business, that all of our other services were simply supportive of our book distribution, including our harināma-saṅkīrtana.

In this way, Śrīla Prabhupāda showed me something about himself that I had never seen before. He took me to his chest, and I had my head on his shoulder and I was crying and crying, and he was patting my head, and he was telling me, "It's all right, it's all right! You do it very nicely!" And then the dream broke and I woke up.

Later, as I was beginning to explain, three years ago, I had many dreams with Śrīla Prabhupāda coming and giving me various instructions. But in this dream, Prabhupada said something which I felt was very profound and I don't mind sharing with you, even though it may sound very revolutionary. Prabhupada began by telling me, "Actually, book distribution is not enough." Now just try to understand the direction of this instruction. Prabhupada said, "Actually, book distribution is not enough. Our real business is to become bhajanānandī." This may sound like a shock to many devotees, but if you gather your intelligence and analyze the constituents of the instruction that I am going to relate to you, that Prabhupada gave me in this dream, hopefully you'll be able to understand. He said, "Actually, book distribution is not enough. Our real business is to become bhajanānandī. And by our personal example, try to encourage as many others as possible to also become bhajanānandī. Book distribution simply facilitates this."

Try to understand the depth of that instruction, please, and see it in relationship to Bhaktisiddhānta Sarasvatī Ṭhākura's instruction that, "The best goṣṭhyānandī is a bhajanānandī who preaches." When we talk of ānandī – ānandī means one who has ānanda. One who experiences ānanda, his bhajana is called a bhajana-ānandī.

There are different stages of realization of the Absolute Truth. There is the anna-maya stage of the realization of the truth. That is the relatively animalistic stage of realizing the truth in filling the belly. Just like for a baby, the only truth that he realizes is the breast of his mother. This stage of anna-maya is characterized by economic development to solve the chapati problems, to fill everybody's belly. Because after all, the army runs on its belly. To keep the cooks fired up so that they would be inspired to continue cooking for the saṅkīrtana devotees who were going out for book distribution, we used to say, "The army runs on its belly!"

The ISKCON army also runs on its belly, but we should be very careful that we don't gravitate, or degenerate, to the anna-maya platform of rather than eating to live – live means preach, life means to preach – eating to live. Rather than eating to live, we live to eat. If we are distributing books just so that we can collect some money to fill our bellies, then we should understand that we are on a very low platform of Kṛṣṇa consciousness. If the Society becomes so concerned for economic development so that we can meet our monthly overheads, then we should understand that we are deviating from the actual direction and purpose of our missionary activities.

Then, after the anna-maya platform, there is the platform called prāṇa-maya – that means to realize the truth in the continuity of one's life. Continuity means continuation of one's life as per the inward and outward-going breaths of the body, the physical body. Prāṇa – prāṇa-maya.

Prāṇa-maya means to realize the truth. We are talking about how there are different aspects, five aspects or five stages, of realization of the Absolute Truth. The first one is realized in foodstuff, filling the belly, economic development. The next stage is when, after one's belly is sufficiently full and he is feeling a little comfortable, he wants to maintain his status quo.

It is characterized by the defense mechanism.

Prāṇa-maya means that he realizes the truth in the continuity of his life's breath – maintenance. This is characterized by an attachment for position. Sometimes, if one sets himself up in a good position, either as a leader or as a manager, or even if he is just the manager of the bathroom cleaning department, we feel secure. And in that security, we know that we are going to get our bellies full because we are doing some service which is recognized by the temple authorities or whatever, and they are not going to kick us out because we are not doing anything practical. The GBC won't strip us of our stripes, so to speak – if you can understand that at all.

These are all types of material consciousness, or external consciousness, and many times it is seen that the prākṛta-bhakta, or the materialistic devotee, very neophyte devotees, they are absorbed in this kind of consciousness in the context of their attempts to advance in devotional service. On the plea of engaging in devotional service or devotional association, there is a tendency to gravitate toward the fulfillment of such lower motivations on the material platform.

After the prāṇa-maya platform, there is mano-maya. Mano-maya means the mental platform, wherein one tries to justify, or rationalize, his existence. And so we create various types of "isms" or philosophies that support our particular world view. Then beyond that is jñāna-maya or vijñāna-maya. That's when one begins to understand the distinction between the body and the self. He begins to actually perceive the reality of the distinction between matter and spirit, and he is able to clearly distinguish between material and spiritual activities. And on the basis of this vijñāna-maya, when the vijñāna-maya platform of realization is infused with the kṛpā, Guru-kṛṣṇa-prasāde pāya bhakti-latā-bīja. When bhakti is infused in the heart of such a jñānī or vijñānī, that is called the ānanda-maya platform, because ānanda can only come from the execution of pure devotional service.

In this way, the real bhajanānandī is one who has achieved the ānanda-māyā platform of life, wherein he is actually relishing ānanda – that means ānanda which is based on rasa – what is called prema-ānanda, on the basis of his realization of sa guṇān samatītyaitān brahma-bhūyāya kalpate, on the spiritual platform.

Other practitioners, madhyama-adhikārīs, who are steadily engaged in the practices of pure devotional service in pursuit of the ānanda-māyā platform, may also be understood to be ānandīs or bhajanānandīs, but they are not perfect in their realization of the ānanda-māyā platform. They are practicing to express their love for Kṛṣṇa, to make friendships with the Vaiṣṇavas, and to do mercy upon innocent fallen conditioned souls or more fallen conditioned souls, and to avoid the demons. They are careful to protect their progressive march to the ānanda-maya platform. So that status may also be termed as Vaiṣṇava or ānandī.

A real bhajanānandī is one who takes pleasure in the pursuit of prema-ānanda by executing the processes of bhajana-kriyā. Bhajana-kriyā – bhajana-ānandī.

ādau śraddhā tataḥ sādhu-
saṅgo 'tha bhajana-kriyā
tato 'nartha-nivṛttiḥ syāt
tato niṣṭhā rucis tataḥ
athāsaktis tato bhāvas
tataḥ premābhyudañcati
sādhakānām ayaṁ premṇaḥ
prādurbhāve bhavet kramaḥ
(Bhakti-rasāmṛta-sindhu 1.4.15–16)

Bhajana-kriyā! One who delights in pursuing the principle of prema, cultivating the desire to give pleasure to the senses of Kṛṣṇa, is also considered to be a bhajana-kriya-ānandī, bhajanānandī. As far as bhajana is concerned, Śrīla Prabhupāda has instructed that kīrtana is our bhajana. Because all the ācāryas agree that the performance of kīrtana, specifically nāma-kīrtana and more specifically nāma-saṅkīrtana, is the most important and the most powerful form of all the aṅgas, or limbs, of devotional service.

In Kali-yuga no other limb of devotional service can give its fullest result without the performance of saṅkīrtana. The performance of saṅkīrtana is inclusive of all other aṅgas of devotional service. We get to hear the name of Kṛṣṇa. We get to chant the name of Kṛṣṇa. We get to remember the name of Kṛṣṇa, serve the name of Kṛṣṇa, worship the name of Kṛṣṇa, be friends with the name of Kṛṣṇa, and surrender everything to the name of Kṛṣṇa. The name of Kṛṣṇa is also inclusive of His rūpa, His guṇa, and His līlā. This is very essential for devotees who are essence-seeking devotees. There are two types of devotees: essence-seeking devotees and ass-like, mūḍha-like, load-carrying devotees. The essence-seeking devotees are those who are seeking essential truths.

The most essential truth is to understand that the science of self-realization culminates in realizing ourselves as parts and parcels of the pleasure potency, or compassionate nature, of Kṛṣṇa. Śrīmatī Rādhārāṇī is the personification of the compassionate nature of Kṛṣṇa, as described by Rūpa Gosvāmī in the Bhakti-rasāmṛta-sindhu. We are parts and parcels of that pleasure potency. As such, the conclusion should be drawn that we are part and parcel of the compassionate nature of Kṛṣṇa. It is the very intrinsic quality of the soul, the dharma of the soul, to be compassionate. That will have its – as we were describing in one previous discussion – it will have its external feature in the matter of reaching out to the fallen souls to help them to have a chance to go back home, back to Godhead, or to meet with Kṛṣṇa, and it will have its internal feature, which is to express that compassion in the form of facilitating the meeting of Rādhā and Kṛṣṇa.

In order to invoke, or realize, awaken, the very intrinsic nature of the Self, in order to actually become self-realized, it is necessary for us to make efforts to express that compassion. Especially in the beginning of our devotional service, it must be expressed in terms of the external aspect, or the external direction of our compassion in the matter of helping others to come to Kṛṣṇa consciousness. Just like Śrīla Prabhupāda told us that in the maṅgala-ārati, if we are feeling sleepy and sluggish and don't feel the inspiration or the ecstasy, if we don't feel ecstatic enough to dance and chant in the maṅgala-ārati, then what to do? What to do is that you dance and chant in the maṅgala-ārati, and by dancing and chanting, you'll get out of the doldrums and begin to feel inspired and experience the happiness of dancing and chanting in the kīrtana.

Similarly, in order to experience, or realize, what it means to be a pure devotee, we have to act like the pure devotees act! It is not a question of being pre-cut. It is a question of desiring perfection. If one wants to become perfect, then he has to act as the perfect souls are acting – but not in all respects. There is what is called anukaraṇa, which means to follow the activities of the great souls, and then there is anusaraṇa. Anusaraṇa means to follow them by surrendering to their principles, to surrender to their instructions. We may not be able, in our present condition as neophytes, to immediately run out in the dead of night and join Kṛṣṇa in the rāsa dance. We may not have the spiritual body with which to embrace Kṛṣṇa and kiss Kṛṣṇa and all these things, or to dance with Kṛṣṇa, etc., but we do have the right to embrace Kṛṣṇa by embracing His principles. On the absolute platform, there is no difference between Kṛṣṇa and Kṛṣṇa's principles. There is no difference between Kṛṣṇa and Kṛṣṇa's instructions. So by heartfeltedly embracing the instructions of guru and Kṛṣṇa in practical effect, we are awakening the real adhikāra for embracing Kṛṣṇa. And this is most effectively achieved by performance of harināma-saṅkīrtana in relationship to hearing about Kṛṣṇa's rūpa, guṇa, and līlā.

We may chant the Holy Name, but there is also need for conception. If we don't have the concept of the actual definition of the Holy Name, then our chanting may not advance very rapidly. Or the chanting may be easily diverted to some other meditation, a meditation that is not favorable for the cultivation of the ultimate goal of our bhajana, which is kṛṣṇa-prema. Prabhupāda has always instructed us that the goal of our bhajana is kṛṣṇa-prema. In this regard, I should read a statement by Śrīla Prabhupāda in his book, which he considers to be the A, B, C, D´s of the cultivation of Kṛṣṇa consciousness. Before we start the Bhāgavatam class, we should hear a little something from the Bhagavad-gītā. This is just a preamble.

I'll have you know that this instruction is found in the very height of Śrīla Prabhupāda's personal ecstasies found in the purports of the eighteenth chapter of the Bhagavad-gītā, in the very two most essential instructions of Kṛṣṇa in the Bhagavad-gītā. There are two most essential instructions of Kṛṣṇa in the Bhagavad-gītā. The first one is:

man-manā bhava mad-bhakto
mad-yājī māṁ namaskuru
mām evaiṣyasi satyaṁ te
pratijāne priyo ,si me
(Bhagavad-gītā 18.65)

The second one is:

sarva-dharmān parityajya
māṁ ekaṁ śaraṇaṁ vraja
ahaṁ tvāṁ sarva-pāpebhyo
mokṣayiṣyāmi mā śucaḥ
(Bhagavad-gītā 18.66)

And Kṛṣṇa says that one who explains these instructions to the devotees, that for him, pure devotional service is guaranteed and there is never anyone more dear, never will there ever be anyone more dear than he who explains – what? Who explains these two most essential instructions of the Gītā, which are meant to solidify our śraddhā at the lotus feet of none other than Kṛṣṇa. So listen to this purport, please. This statement of Śrīla Prabhupāda will help to at least partially answer your question that you asked me in my room yesterday. Pūrṇacandra Prabhu asked me a question regarding the substantiation of the concept that we are meant for vraja-bhakti, that all jīvas are meant for vraja-bhakti.

Please remember that in our previous discussion, we mentioned that Kṛṣṇa instructed Arjuna that māṁ ekaṁ śaraṇaṁ vraja. Vraja meaning "to go," but where to go is indicated in the word vraja itself, to surrender to Him there and we discussed how it is that Arjuna took that instruction very seriously to heart and he actually in fact went to Vraja in the form of Arjunīyā Gopī. He was transformed into a gopī and experienced love dalliances in Kṛṣṇa's association. Arjuna was a friend of Kṛṣṇa, and he was a warrior and a family man and all these things, yet Kṛṣṇa is instructing him to go to Vraja.

Similarly, just hear this instruction of Śrīla Prabhupāda in his purport to verse 65 of the Eighteenth Chapter of the Bhagavad-gītā. This is a very profound and insightful instruction which should not be allowed to pass us by unnoticed:

man-manā bhava mad-bhakto
mad-yājī māṁ namaskuru
mām evaiṣyasi satyaṁ te
pratijāne priyo ,si me

"Always think of Me, become My devotee, worship Me and offer your homage unto Me. Thus, you will come to Me without fail. I promise you this because you are My very dear friend."

Purport: "The most confidential part of knowledge is that one should become a pure devotee of Kṛṣṇa." He is not saying in this purport that one should become a devotee of Nārāyaṇa, nor is he saying that one should become a devotee of Varāha, nor a pure devotee of Matsya, Nṛsiṁha, Śiva – any of these things. He is saying that the most confidential part of knowledge is that one should become a pure devotee of Kṛṣṇa and always think of Him and act for Him. "One should not become an official meditator. Rather, life should be so molded that one will always have the chance to think of Kṛṣṇa."

"Official meditator" should be explained a little. That means that you meditate on Kṛṣṇa or you meditate on void or whatever for a few minutes – or even meditating on Kṛṣṇa for a few minutes, and then for the rest of the day go on with your nonsense. "But rather, one's whole life" – I'm adding these words – "rather one's whole life." He is saying, "Life should be so molded," but it should be understood: rather than becoming an official meditator, meditating and then going on with nonsense, rather your whole life, twenty-four hours a day, "should be so molded that one will always have the chance to think of Kṛṣṇa. One should always act in such a way that all his daily activities are in connection with Kṛṣṇa."

After all, please remember that this is the Kṛṣṇa consciousness movement. It is not the other-aspects-of-Godhead consciousness movement, but rather it is the Kṛṣṇa consciousness movement. Vṛndāvana is the home of Kṛṣṇa, and Vṛndāvana is also the home of our own spiritual master, who has spread the Kṛṣṇa consciousness movement, or the Vṛndāvana consciousness movement. He should arrange his life in such a way that throughout the twenty-four hours, he cannot but think of Kṛṣṇa.

Please – it doesn't take much brains to understand that this book is meant to be distributed to every living entity on this planet practically, and they are to read this and take this instruction seriously. And the Lord's promise is that anyone who is in such pure Kṛṣṇa consciousness will certainly return to the abode of Kṛṣṇa, where he will be engaged in the association of Kṛṣṇa face to face. Not any other Kṛṣṇa, please!

"This most confidential part of knowledge is spoken to Arjuna because he is the dear friend of Kṛṣṇa." Of course, one may argue at this point that he was the dear friend of Vāsudeva-Kṛṣṇa, not Vrajendra-nandana Kṛṣṇa, but please remember our previous discussion about how Arjuna attained the supreme perfection by the grace of his guru. Vāsudeva-Kṛṣṇa was acting as his guru, and He instructed Arjuna to take shelter of Kṛṣṇa in Vraja. And Arjuna did so and attained the supreme perfection of realization of his gopī-deha in the vraja-līlā. So that should be kept in mind in relationship to this discussion, please.

This little insight information is required to complete the picture considerably. "Everyone who follows the path of Arjuna …" What path did he take in order to attain the perfection, to follow the instruction māṁ ekaṁ śaraṇaṁ vraja? By following that instruction, he followed that path. And so Prabhupāda is saying, "Anyone who follows the path of Arjuna can become a dear friend of Kṛṣṇa and attain the same perfection as Arjuna."

Arjuna was a friend, and he desired to become a gopī. Prabhupāda did say that it is possible, although it generally doesn't happen, but it is possible for one to change his rasa. But that's another discussion, which would require considerable time.

Listen now, please listen. I'm begging you with folded hands, please listen. "These words stress that one" – "one" is first-person active – it is meant to induce the reader to act on this, the very reader. Whoever is reading, anyone who is reading – to act on the instruction which is being given. "These words stress that one should concentrate his mind on Kṛṣṇa, the very form with two hands, carrying a flute."

Vāsudeva-Kṛṣṇa doesn't carry a flute. Nārāyaṇa doesn't carry a flute. I never saw a picture of Varāha carrying a flute, and certainly I don't know how much He would be able hold the flute between his hooves. "These words stress that one should concentrate his mind upon Kṛṣṇa, the very form with two hands, carrying a flute, the bluish boy with a beautiful face and peacock feathers in His hair."

We hear that Nārāyaṇa doesn't wear peacock feathers. We hear that when the Kṛṣṇa who left Vṛndāvana, when He left Vṛndāvana, He threw off His peacock feather. He gave His flute to Rādhārāṇī and the sakhīs. Vāsudeva-Kṛṣṇa is killing demons and other such activities, establishing religious principles and all these things, but He is not playing the flute.

It is Vrajendra-nandana Kṛṣṇa who plays the flute. It is Vrajendra-nandana Kṛṣṇa who wears the peacock feathers in His hair, and also Rādhārāṇī wears peacock feathers in Her hair.

And even the cowherd boys sometimes wear peacock feathers in their hair. That is the symbol of the land of Vraja – the beautiful simple rural cowherd setting, where there is dancing of peacocks.

There are descriptions of Kṛṣṇa found in the Brahma-saṁhitā. This is describing the Kṛṣṇa of Goloka from the Brahma-saṁhitā, where He is surrounded by millions of gopīs. Other literatures, such as Bṛhad-bhāgavatāmṛta and also the Padma Purāṇa and Bhāgavata Purāṇa, Govinda-līlāmṛta, Śrī Kṛṣṇa-bhāvanāmṛta, and so many other literatures which are given to us by our ācāryas, describe Vrajendra-nandana Kṛṣṇa.

Now please listen to this one! "One should fix his mind." "One" – first person active – that means you! You should do this! The reader should do this. Whoever gets this book should do this! If he wants his supreme benefit by following the very A, B, C's of spiritual life, please! These are the A, B, C's. If you can't even get pass the A, B, C's, then how you are going to understand the E, F, G's and the X, Y, Z's? So first we have to understand the A, B, C's, and this instruction is the quintessential instruction of Śrīla Prabhupāda's A, B, C introductory course in this purport.

"One" means the reader, you – "one" – the hearer. "One should fix his mind on this original form, svayam ..." "Original" means svayam, "form" means rūpa. "One should fix his mind on this svayaṁ-rūpa, or original form of Godhead, Kṛṣṇa. One should not ..." Listen to this one, please! Here is the punch line, all right? "One should not even divert his attention to other forms of the Lord. The Lord has multi-forms as Viṣṇu, Nārāyaṇa, Rāma, Varāha, etc." I mean, Prabhupāda is spelling it right out. It's not so difficult to grasp the direction of his instruction. Varāha, etc. Etcetera means "and so on and so forth." In other words, you can continue the string of incarnations and manifestations of Godhead ad infinitum by this word of etcetera.

"The Lord has multi-forms as Viṣṇu, Nārāyaṇa, Rāma, Varāha, etc., but a devotee should concentrate his mind on the form that was present before Arjuna" [laughing]. The form present before Arjuna in his form as Arjunīyā Gopi. He wasn't present before Arjuna in the two-handed form, playing a flute and with peacock feathers, but Prabhupāda is instructing that we should concentrate on this form, with two hands, carrying the flute and with a peacock feather.

And he says, "the very form with two hands carrying a flute. The bluish boy, the bluish boy with a beautiful face and peacock feathers." So it indicates His childhood pastimes in Vraja. "Concentration of the mind on the form of Kṛṣṇa constitutes the most confidential part of knowledge, and this is disclosed to Arjuna because Arjuna is the most dear friend of Kṛṣṇa."

Anyway, we don't want to extrapolate too much our own ideas into Śrīla Prabhupāda's purport, but I do think – in certain respects – that if you take this into consideration, we do have rights to express our own heart's feelings. And this is not in disagreement with the teachings of our predecessor ācāryas. Our predecessor ācāryas and Śrīla Prabhupāda also in his purports advocate that one should concentrate on this form of Kṛṣṇa, with two hands, carrying the flute and with a peacock feather. After all, he has mentioned "original form," svayaṁ-rūpa. There is svayaṁ-rūpa, svayaṁ-prakāśa, vilāsa-vigraha, and so many other forms of Godhead.

Our ācāryas – Viśvanātha Cakravartī Ṭhākura, Bhaktivinoda Ṭhākura, Bhaktisiddhānta, and Prabhupāda also – all agree that all the expanded forms of Kṛṣṇa up to the svayaṁ-prakāśa manifestations, who expanded to dance by the side of each gopī in the mahā-rāsa, all of them have only up to 93 percent of the beauty, sweetness, and lovableness of Godhead. Therefore, they always give stress to the meditation and absorption of our heart in the service of the svayaṁ-rūpa Kṛṣṇa, who is Rādhārāṇī's Kṛṣṇa, Rādhā-Kṛṣṇa.

The whole section of this chapter from the book Śrī Kṛṣṇa-samhita by Srila Bhaktivinoda Ṭhākura is very pertinent to this discussion. This is Chapter 9: "Achievement of the Lotus Feet of Lord Kṛṣṇa." Before we open the questions, we can just read part of this paragraph. This is Text 12, page 142. I'll begin with a short text, number 1:

ākarṣaṇa-svarūpeṇa
vaṁśī gītena sundaraḥ
mādaren viśvam etad vai
gopīnām-aharan-manaḥ

"Lord Śrī Kṛṣṇa, who is realized through samādhi ..." Bhaktivinoda Ṭhākura here in this book, he is defining samādhi as devotional service. Practical devotional service while we have the sādhaka-deha in this world, and prīti, or loving devotional service, in the siddha-deha. "Lord Śrī Kṛṣṇacandra, who is realized through samādhi, kidnaps the hearts of the gopīs and maddens the spiritual and the material worlds with the sound of His flute, which is the form of all attraction."

jātyādi-mada-vibhrāntyā
kṛṣṇāptir durhṛdām kutaḥ
gopīnām kevalam kṛṣṇaś
cittam ākarṣaṇe kṣamaḥ

Text 12: "How can those, whose hearts have been polluted…" Here we come into conditional consciousness. "How can those, whose hearts have been polluted by social prestige, attain Kṛṣṇa?"

"The wicked pride of this material world has six causes." We are talking about the cause of pride. "Birth, beauty, qualities, knowledge, opulence, and bodily strength. People who are overwhelmed by these six kinds of pride cannot take to the devotional service of the Lord. We are experiencing this every day in our life. Persons who are polluted by the pride of knowledge consider the science of Kṛṣṇa very insignificant. While considering the goal of life, such people regard the happiness of Brahman to be superior to the happiness of devotional service. Persons who are devoid of pride attain the mood of gopas and gopīs to enjoy with Kṛṣṇa. The gopas and gopīs are the authorities in the science of Kṛṣṇa."

In the Sanskrit text, the word gopīs is used. So he is explaining, "The reason for using the word gopī in this verse is that in this book we are discussing the topmost rasa of conjugal love. Persons who are situated in śānta-, dāsya-, sakhya-, and vātsalya-rasas are also in the mood of Vraja, and they realize the transcendental mellows in relationship with Kṛṣṇa according to the respective moods. We are not going to elaborate on them in this book. Actually, all living entities are eligible for the mood of Vraja. When one's heart is filled with the mood of mādhurya, he attains Vraja in full perfection. Out of the five rasas, a person is naturally attracted to the rasa in which he has an eternal constitutional relationship with the Lord, and he should therefore worship the Lord in that particular mood. But in this book, we have described only the living entity's topmost mood of conjugal love." So there you have it. We are going to open for a few questions now.

Pūrṇacandra Prabhu: I accept, in one sense, that all living entities can certainly become eligible, but we also have to know where ... and because we know that out of the one thousand mahā-yugas, in only one of them that Kṛṣṇa and Mahāprabhu Himself propagate that vraja-bhakti. In all the other mahā-yugas, all the living entities, they are worshiping different forms of Nārāyaṇa. So how do we put it together?

Aindra Prabhu: I can share with you a few ideas from this subject matter. And the first point is that if we will actually take a look at the kingdom of God, we have to first of all understand that this material word is ekapāda-vibhūti and the spiritual world is tripāda-vibhūti. And that is meant to show how less significant the material world is in terms of the degradation of the jīva. In other words, the prison house is much smaller than the real world, like a "pre-world." This is to show that we, as conditioned souls in this material world, are not the majority. In other words, majority rules, not that the minority rules. If you are going to take a decision by majority-vote, then the majority rules. Majority decides.

There are descriptions in the ācāryas' commentaries on the Bhakti-rasāmṛta-sindhu how this kingdom of God is set up. The material world on this side of the

Virajā river comprises a very small segment of the kingdom of God. Yet there are innumerable living entities, practically uncountable living entities, even within one cubic inch of air. Within this material world, there is a living entity and a jīva and Paramātmā also within every atom of the creation, aside from the fact that there are many atoms which are comprising every physical body. Each physical body will be having other physical bodies within it, such as parasites, etc. like in a human body or in a horse's body.

So really, it is impossible for any human being to imagine, or to conceive, of how many living entities there are even in this material world. However, it is stated that the whorl of the kingdom of God is the realm of Vraja on the Goloka planet. And outside of that whorl is the realm of Mathurā.

Outside of that realm – it is described like this. There may be different descriptions in different places, but it is shown like this in this particular description by Jīva Gosvāmī and his commentaries on the Bhakti-rasāmṛta-sindhu. So outside of Mathurā is the realm of Dvārakā. And outside the realm of Dvārakā, on the Goloka-vṛndāvana planet, is a realm called Vaikuṇṭha-vṛndāvana, or Goloka.

We are going progressively outside on the Goloka-vṛndāvana planet. Outside the realm of Dvārakā is the realm of Goloka-vṛndāvana, or Vaikuṇṭha-vṛndāvana, where Lord Kṛṣṇa is worshiped in awe and reference, reverential devotion, or vaidhī-bhakti. Vaikuṇṭha-vṛndāvana means where Kṛṣṇa is worshiped in His majestic aspect. It is Kṛṣṇaloka, but in Kṛṣṇaloka there is Vrajendra-nandana Kṛṣṇa, Mathurā-Kṛṣṇa, Dvārkādīśa-Kṛṣṇa, and Vaikuṇṭhanātha, Goloka-Kṛṣṇa.

Then outside that is the realm of Puruṣottama-dhāma. And then outside of that is the realm of Ayodhya. Then, outside of that are the Vaikuṇṭhalokas. Then there is the Virajā river. And outside of that is this material realm, the mahat-tattva. Puruṣottama-dhāma is the original prototype of Puruṣottama-kṣetra, found as Jagannātha Purī in this world. You can read about that in Bṛhad-bhāgavatāmṛta when Gopa Kumara goes there and he was discussing with Nārada Muni and Uddhava, and Nārada is recommending that he go to Puruṣottama-dhāma to do his bhajana there, and Uddhava is objecting, saying that it will not be possible for him to have the humility which is required to actually perfect his Vraja-bhajana if he goes to Puruṣottama-dhāma on account of the admixture of aiśvarya in that realm. So therefore, he should resort to Vraja-bhūmi and complete his course of Kṛṣṇa consciousness by doing bhajana in Vraja-bhūmi, which is the topmost bhajana-sthāna.

I am bringing this point up in relationship to your question because in the analysis given by the ācārya, he tells that if you will take all the realms and all the numerous living entities in all these different realms of the material world – Devī-dhāma, Maheśa-dhāma, Hari-dhāma, means Vaikuṇṭha, Goloka-vṛndāvana, meaning Vaikuṇṭha-vṛndāvana, Dvārakā, and Mathurā – if you'll add all these realms in terms of their expansions and in terms of the numbers of living entities' population of these different realms, if you will put them all together, it will not begin to approach the expansiveness and the population of the realm of Vraja.

Prabhupāda says in a Bhāgavatam purport that it is possible to be elevated from the Vaikuṇṭhalokas to Goloka. That means that you will not be carrying your vaikuṇṭha-svarūpa with you anymore than you will necessarily carry your Earthly svarūpa with you to Vaikuṇṭha, although it may be possible to go there in the selfsame body. But it is possible to elevate from one realm to another.

Just like we are called nitya-baddha-jīvas, but it is not actually nitya in the sense that it will be considered to be an eternal conditional file. One can be elevated from this material world, which is also a compartment of the kingdom of God, to another compartment which is of a higher spiritual order. So similarly, one can also be elevated from a lower spiritual order to a higher spiritual order.

First of all, the realm of Vraja is the majority – the realm of Vraja rules. Kṛṣṇa doesn't interfere with the free will of the living entity. He may inspire or try to inspire in one way or another, but we see that it is due to desire that living entities have come to this material world. It is due to their individual execution of their minute independence. Similarly, it is due to desire that one remains doggedly attached to this material world, in spite of the fact that the best rasika Vaiṣṇavas are preaching all over the world. They disregard, or they refuse to allow themselves to be influenced by their merciful propaganda.

We can say that it is a rare achievement, but that is only because the conditioning of the living entity is so deeply rooted in various ways. We can say that the achievement of vraja-bhakti is a rare achievement, but that is because the conditioning of the living entity is so deeply rooted in various ways. Ei rūpe brahmāṇḍa bhramite kona bhāgyavān jīva guru-kṛṣṇa-prasāde pāya vraja-bhakti-latā-bīja. (Śrī Caitanya-caritāmṛta, Madhya-līlā 19.151)

There are two things required: There is this need for an empowered or powerful representative of Kṛṣṇa, and there is need for the receptivity of the individual soul. All living entities, as mentioned here, have the eligibility for the moods of Vraja, but why is it that one living entity is squirming through a stool of a hog as a worm and another living entity is as a demigod and doggedly attached to that? Why is it that one living entity is taking his birth on one loka at a particular time and another living entity is taking birth on another loka at another time?

Why is it that one living entity is bhukti-kāmī and another living entity is mukti-kāmī? Some desire the brahma-sāyujya, sāyujya-mukti, and others may even desire sālokya-mukti, sārṣṭi-mukti, and all these things. Those living entities who are taking their birth on Earth or in various lokas at certain times, it is due to their saṁskāras, or it is due to their accumulated piety, it is due to their sukṛti, it is due to their levels of faith, which have manifest in the course of their sojourn through material existence. It is due to their desires. And because Kṛṣṇa doesn't interfere with their desires, and because Kṛṣṇa easily gives bhukti and mukti, since He is the friend of all living entities. Suhṛdaṁ sarva-bhūtānāṁ jñātvā māṁ śāntim ṛcchati.

Suhṛdaṁ sarva-bhūtānāṁ means that He is the friend of all living entities. And because He is the friend of all living entities, He acts to fulfill everyone's desires. So, someone may be taking their birth in Satya-yuga or Tretā-yuga, or in the Dvāpara-yuga or Kali-yuga. This is not by chance, but rather it is on account of the fact that these living entities have accumulated various degrees of sukṛti and formulated within their hearts various conceptions, which augment various desires.

Prabhupāda has told that Kṛṣṇa is so kind that if you have a pinch of material desire in your heart, that He is so kind that He will make the arrangements for you get another material body with which to pursue your paltry, disgusting, reprehensible pinch of material desire. You become so attached to something that you can't see the value of something of a higher order. That's why many times when we preach about Kṛṣṇa consciousness, it goes over people's heads. They can't grasp the idea of it, because they are so much entangled in their own paltry little small world of sense gratification. And it's very difficult to break them loose from their attachments.

Similarly, since various standards of desires are manifesting in various living entities' hearts due to their associations and various other factors, a desire for liberation may come to the living entity. And Kṛṣṇa is so merciful that He appears like He appears to Gajendra in the gajendra-mokṣa-līlā. He appears, and various other examples are there where the Personality of Godhead, who grants mukti to them, appears to fulfill their desires and takes them to a better situation than the situation they are in.

It is just like, when Kaṁsa was killed, he got a better situation. When Śiśupāla was killed, he got a better situation. In other words, Kṛṣṇa is always acting for the benefit of all the living entities. He doesn't want them to rot in the material existence.

Better to give them at least a space where they can be freed from material suffering. Kṛṣṇa comes once in the day of Brahmā to fulfill the desires of those who have accumulated sufficient sukṛti to take advantage of His topmost association that He has to give from the standpoint of the majority-rule.

You'll find that in this material world it's very difficult, almost next to impossible. You will have to shed liters and liters of blood just to even get one person to abandon his attachment to the pursuit of material sense gratification to even take up vaidhī-bhakti. What to speak of actually getting them to truly appreciate the beauty of the topmost thing?

It is stated how rare the attainment of vraja-bhakti and the realm of vraja-bhakti is. When our ācāryas make this point that it is so rarely achieved, that is to try to impress upon the reader that, "Here is your golden opportunity!" Who cares for what happened in Satya-yuga? Who cares for what happened in Tretā-yuga?

Who cares for what happened really in Dvāpara-yuga? The fact that a few people were elevated śruti-cārīs and muni-cārīs, śruti-devīs, and Daṇḍakāraṇya-ṛṣis were elevated to gopī-bhāva, that does not have much to do with us, because we are still entrenched in the muck of material existence, although it may serve as an inspiration and induce us to leave this realm – but who cares for it?

Here it is: You have taken your birth – you are one of the rare few – so don't abandon this opportunity! Don't miss! And even if we will take all the human beings on this planet and induce them all to become devotees of Rādhā and Kṛṣṇa, still, in relationship to all the other living entities in this universe, or even all the other living entities on this planet, what to speak of all the other living entities in all the other universes! Compared to all these other living entities, the very, very few living entities or human beings who reside on this planet constitutes rarity in the matter of who gets the opportunity.

Kṛṣṇa Candra Prabhu (on behalf of another Russian devotee in the audience): It is a well-known statement that Śrīla Prabhupāda once said, "I would prefer to die on the battlefield like Arjuna while preaching." How to understand this? Because in this statement it is very difficult to see this mood, like that of Vraja. So how to understand that?

Aindra Prabhu: Oh, Hare Kṛṣṇa! This is a good question. However, it really isn't so difficult to understand if you understand Prabhupāda's internal mood. Just like we see Prahlāda Mahārāja is expressing in the Bhagavad-gītā that he has no anxiety himself, but he is anxious for the fools and rascals who are absorbed in material sense gratification. He only wants to save them and make them happy in Kṛṣṇa consciousness. It's just like within dāsya-rasa is śānta-rasa. Within sakhya-rasa is dāsya-rasa and śānta-rasa. Within vātsalya-rasa is sakhya-, dāsya-, and śānta-rasa. And within mādhurya-rasa, there is vātsalya-, sakhya-, dāsya-, and śānta-rasa. The things which are to be seen in the lower order will also be seen in their highest perfection in the higher order.

The example is that every number is based on the numerical number one. One is also included in two. And one is also included in ten. One hundred, one thousand, one million, one billion. One is also included in every other subsequent number. Without first understanding one, then you can hardly hope to understand one million. So in the same way, we first have to understand Arjuna's determination to satisfy Kṛṣṇa by fighting on His behalf for re-establishing religious principles, and as a manifestation of compassion. Arjuna is exemplifying that compassionate nature by establishing, for the benefit of all jīvas, for the benefit of the world, the righteous rule of the son of Dharmarāja, Yudhiṣṭhira Mahārāja. So similarly, we see that there is that compassionate nature within Prahlāda Mahārāja. They are devotees of a lower order than the vraja-vāsīs – no doubt!

But if you can't understand the principle as it is displayed in a differentiated way in relation to the devotees of the lower order, how are you going to understand or recognize the same principle in the devotees of a higher order?

We should understand that Śrīla Prabhupāda is a devotee of the highest order. He is a vraja-vāsī, and as a vraja-vāsī, he has the topmost degree of compassion. Please remember that Lord Caitanya is Rādhā and Kṛṣṇa, and that more merciful than Lord Caitanya is Lord Nityānanda. Lord Nityānanda is the manifestation of guru-tattva, and He relishes all five rasas in His services to Lord Caitanya. He also relishes the mādhurya-bhāva. Just as Kṛṣṇa, in the form of Lord Caitanya, relishes the mādhurya-bhāva, so also Balarāma in the form of Nitāi relishes the mādhurya-bhāva. He relishes the mādhurya-bhāva in the form of His svarūpa-śakti manifestation, Anaṅga-mañjarī. Anaṅga-mañjarī is the younger sister of Rādhārāṇī and the closest associate of Srimati Rādhārāṇī. So similarly, the closest associate of Lord Caitanya is Lord Nityānanda. He is the mercy manifestation of Lord Caitanya in the same way that Anaṅga-mañjarī is ādi-guru in the mādhurya-rasa and is the mercy manifestation of Śrīmatī Rādhārāṇī. She acts as the liaison between the jīvas who aspire for the service of Rādhā, and Śrīmatī Rādhārāṇī Herself. Therefore, it is said, heno nitāi bine bhāi, rādhā-kṛṣṇa pāite nāi. Without getting the mercy of Lord Nityānanda, who is the embodiment of the very guru-tattva in all rasas, including the mādhurya-rasa, one cannot have entrance into the service of Rādhā and Kṛṣṇa.

We should not forget that Śrīla Prabhupāda is a śaktyāveśa-avatāra of nityānanda-svarūpa-śakti. That has been ascertained by many great devotees in our line. Śrīla Prabhupāda is a manifestation of the mercy of Gaura-Nitāi who came to give the highest loving service at the lotus feet of Rādhā and Kṛṣṇa.

Dying on the battlefield like Arjuna means that as a representative of Nityānanda, he will never give up the service of Rādhā and Kṛṣṇa, the service of Lord Caitanya, in the matter of fulfilling Kṛṣṇa's desire to deliver the fallen, conditioned souls to the realm of Vraja.

I have included some quotes from Śrīla Prabhupāda's Caitanya-caritāmṛta purport. This should help to make you understand what Prabhupāda is as a soldier on the field. This is a purport to this verse in Caitanya-caritāmṛta, Madhya-līlā, Chapter 23, Text 104, where Mahāprabhu is instructing Sanātana Gosvāmī.

"Establish devotional service to Lord Kṛṣṇa and Rādhārāṇī in Vṛndāvana. You should also compile bhakti scriptures to preach the bhakti cult from Vṛndāvana." This was Mahāprabhu's instruction to Sanātana Gosvāmī, and this is Śrīla Prabhupāda's purport: "This Kṛṣṇa consciousness movement continues the tradition of the Six Gosvāmīs, especially Śrīla Sanātana Gosvāmī and Śrīla Rūpa Gosvāmī. Serious students of this Kṛṣṇa consciousness movement" – now, here it comes. This is the punctuation, the exclamation point. What serious students of this Kṛṣṇa consciousness movement should do. "Serious students of this Kṛṣṇa consciousness movement MUST (underlined and bold) understand their great responsibility to preach." To preach what? "The cult of Vṛndāvana." To preach the cult of Vṛndāvana.

Dying on the battlefield means preaching the cult of Vṛndāvana, following in the footsteps of Rūpa and Sanātana as representatives of the most merciful manifestation of Śrī Caitanya Mahāprabhu in the form of Nitāi.

"Serious students of this Kṛṣṇa consciousness movement must understand their great responsibility to preach the cult of Vṛndāvana, pure devotional service to the Lord, all over the world. We now have a nice temple in Vṛndāvana, and serious students should take advantage of it." Do you know that Śrīla Prabhupāda instructed that he wanted all of the devotees, all of his disciples, to come to Vṛndāvana at least once a year? I am referring to a letter to Karāndhara, who at that time was in Los Angeles, where the American BBT was located. He says that all disciples must once a year visit Vṛndāvana, and GBC men, sannyāsīs, and preachers should come to Vṛndāvana at least three or four times a year, never mind the expense! That is a direct quote.

Furthermore, listen! Indradyumna Swami said that Prabhupāda told that he wanted that the leaders of this movement should spend at least six month a year in Vṛndāvana! Why? Because they require the śakti to preach the cult – the śakti and the realizations to preach the cult of Vṛndāvana all over the world.

This brings us back to the very beginning of our discussion today – that the best goṣṭhyānandī is a bhajanānandī who preaches. Now, there is one more sentence: "We now have a very nice temple in Vṛndāvana and serious students should take advantage of it. I ..." Śrīla Prabhupāda is saying, "I." The person who is saying "I" is Śrīla Prabhupāda. It is our Śrīla Prabhupāda who is the person who is saying, "I." "I am very hopeful that some of our students can take up this responsibility and render the best service to humanity by educating people in Kṛṣṇa consciousness." Not Nārāyaṇa consciousness.

So are there any other questions?

Kṛṣṇa Candra Prabhu (on behalf of another Russian devotee): Do you have any plans to go outside Vṛndāvana for the purpose of preaching?

Aindra Prabhu: No! If you want to go outside of Vṛndāvana for preaching purposes, I have no objection really. One way of answering that question would be that we have our plans and Kṛṣṇa has His plans. My desire is to satisfy my spiritual master. If my spiritual master has mercifully awarded this Vraja-dhāma as my prabhu-dhatta deśa, my preaching field, then I feel unlimitedly blessed.

I would rather become a worm in the stool of a pig in Vṛndāvana than become a queen of Dvārakā or a resident of Vaikuṇṭha. I rather see the proposition of going to Vaikuṇṭha to be no better than the proposition of going to hell. Vaikuṇṭha without Kṛṣṇa playing His flute and dancing with the gopīs and Śrīmatī Rādhārāṇī is as good as hell. It is my solemn and firm determination that I will always augment the mood of a vraja-vāsī in that I will never ever consider any other mood to be worth my attention even for a half a sesame seed of time.

It is mentioned in Mathurā-māhātmya that anyone who thinks to leave Vṛndāvana and is happy to live anywhere else in this world is a fool who is bewildered by ignorance.

Also, it is mentioned that if after having attained Rādhārāṇī's mercy to place even one foot in this Vraja-maṇḍala, if someone will choose to leave Vraja-maṇḍala for any other reason than to preach the glories of Vṛndāvana-dhāma, to preach the glories of vraja-bhakti, to preach the glories of the vraja-vāsīs all over the world, then he commits the greatest offense against Vṛndāvana-dhāma. The greatest offense against Vṛndāvana-dhāma is to leave Vṛndāvana-dhāma. If someone thinks that all desires, either for bhukti, mukti, or bhakti, cannot be fulfilled in Vṛndāvana-dhāma and goes elsewhere to fulfill those desires, he is a pāṣaṇḍī, a rascal.

The only excusable reason for leaving Vṛndāvana is to leave in the same mood that Śrīla Prabhupāda left – to preach the glories of Vṛndāvana and Vṛndāvana-candra, Kṛṣṇa, and the vraja-gopīs on behalf of Caitanya Mahāprabhu all over the world. In doing so, he doesn't commit any offense in the matter of leaving Vṛndāvana-dhāma because in certain respects, he never leaves Vṛndāvana-dhāma, he never leaves the service of Vṛndāvana-dhāma.

However, I have my own feelings based on certain information that I have acquired on account of my service at the feet of Śrīla Prabhupāda. Śrīla Prabhupāda has instructed that any devotional service which is performed in this Vraja-maṇḍala is a thousand times more powerful or more beneficial than the same devotional service performed anywhere in the world, including

Moscow or any other place in Russia or in America, or wherever. So Śrīla Prabhupāda has instructed that the same devotional service which is performed here is equal a thousand times the benefit of the same devotional service performed anywhere else.

And aside from that, because of various information retrieval systems, it becomes very easy to reach out to the whole world from Vṛndāvana. So if one preaches in Vṛndāvana-dhāma, he gets a thousand times the benefit of preaching. It is as if he has dedicated a thousand lifetimes to Śrīla Prabhupāda's preaching mission. And not only that, but if he can somehow or other be instrumental in helping to induce others to come to Vṛndāvana, to hear his preaching, or to engage in devotional services – to chant, to worship the Deities, to roll in the dust of Vraja, to bathe in Yamunā, to circumambulate Girirāja, and all these things – then those people who come here, they get a thousand times the benefit than what they would get by doing the same activities anywhere else in the world.

If you see the utility in the active intelligent process of going around, traveling, or going here or there for preaching in order to direct other people to the realm of Vraja and help them to take inspiration for coming to Vraja to engage in devotional service here and get a thousand times the benefit, then we have no objection. That is your portfolio. You can take it as your portfolio. Portfolio means your duty as such. You can take that as your duty. And that is also very good.

But Prabhupāda has told that higher than active

intelligence is lazy intelligence. By lazy intelligence, you can sit in one place and with less effort accomplish much more. Prabhupāda instructed that this Vṛndāvana-yātrā is a lazy-intelligent preaching project. That's what he called this Vṛndāvana-yātrā – the lazy intelligent preaching project. We don't have to spend so much money and take so much trouble and so much time for going all over here and there. Rather, in accordance with his instructions, all the devotees of ISKCON should come here.

So if you want to go out and induce others to come here, then you are fulfilling that aspect of Prabhupāda's instructions, but the truth is that there should be someone here to help facilitate the devotees who come here so they can have accessible opportunities for engagement in devotional service by which they can get a thousand times the benefit, which goes into their transcendental bank account.

If I were to go to Russia for example, we would get the benefit of Aindra Dāsa and all of us doing one kīrtana, and I would have to take the trouble to go there. But if you take the trouble, the same trouble that I would have to take to go there to get the benefit of one kīrtana, if you will take the trouble to come here, then we could get the benefit of a thousand kīrtanas!

So why are you asking me to go there? I should be asking you to come here again and again. Because even if I go there, I wouldn't spend the rest of my life there. I would only spend probably a week or so. The devotees try to drag me here and there all over the world.

There is only fifty-two weeks in a year. That

means that out of the hundreds of temples in this society, I'd only be able to visit fifty-two temples. So how many devotees would be benefited by that anyway? And how much benefit would they get out of it? Better that they make a program that all the temples, five hundred temples, or how many temples there are, all of them make a program to regularly, systematically send as many of their devotees to Vṛndāvana-dhāma as possible for a week or two or three, or a month or three months, you know, for festivals. At least if I would be able to only spend a week there, you can come here and spend a week or a month here, and we can get the benefit of a thousand weeks of kīrtana by doing kīrtana here.

If you feel an attachment to your service there, then no problem. But you should understand that it is your foremost duty to encourage as many devotees as possible to come to take shelter of the atmosphere of this Vṛndāvana.

Sometimes devotees will argue that the temple is as good as Vṛndāvana; wherever a temple is, you are as good as being in Vṛndāvana. That may be true, because in Tulasī-māhātmya, it is mentioned that wherever there is one tulasī, that forest in which there is one tulasī is as good as Vṛndāvana. But I would like to suggest that one drop of ocean water is as good as the ocean. We don't deny the qualitative oneness. But we should also not deny the quantitative difference.

If our temple is as good as Vṛndāvana, then why don't we just go sit by the tulasī tree and chant Hare Kṛṣṇa in order to recharge our batteries? Why come to this place to recharge our batteries so that we can go back to the West to preach? Why spend so much money to follow Prabhupāda's instruction to come here at least once a year? And furthermore, why do we have to be so careful to avoid offenses when we are in Vṛndāvana, because when we come to Vṛndāvana, we get a thousand times the reactions to our offenses than we would get if we were chanting beneath a single tulasī tree in our temple. You may be able to do nonsense there and get away with it, or get away with lesser reactions, but when you come here, you have to be very careful so you don't become implicated by dhāma-aparādha. And it's one thousand times reactions.

So we should understand the beauty, the power, the significance, and the privilege of doing devotional service in Vṛndāvana-dhāma and as often as possible resort to Vṛndāvana-dhāma. Resort means come to reside here, take shelter of Vṛndāvana-dhāma. After all, every morning we are praying: Kṛpā kori' koro tāre vṛndāvana-vāsi. Can you understand my point? You should come here at least once a year. Stay for some time, do some serious devotional service, and see how you are rapidly advancing in Kṛṣṇa consciousness. Back home, back to Godhead.

Kṛṣṇa Candra Prabhu: Someone has the same question in relation to Navadvīpa-dhāma.

Aindra Prabhu: Yes, the same question. Śrīla Prabodhānanda Sarasvatī Ṭhākura tells that if your guru instructs you not to reside in Navadvīpa, then he is not your guru. Then in the next verse he says that residing in Navadvīpa constitutes the satisfaction of your guru. So if the guru is not satisfied by your residing in Navadvīpa, then he is not your guru. In other words, he is not the external representative of caitya-guru within your heart. Caitya-guru is fully satisfied when one resides in Navadvīpa-dhāma.

You should understand that Navadvīpa and Vṛndāvana are non-different. Navadvīpa is the audārya aspect of Vṛndāvana. And Vṛndāvana is the mādhurya aspect of Navadvīpa. So the same principle is there. The only difference is that Navadvīpa and Mahāprabhu are very merciful. They give one thousand times the benefit in Navadvīpa, but they don't consider one thousand times the reactions. But it's not that they don't consider any reactions. Those who are offenders will not be able to see the antara-svarūpa of Navadvīpa-dhāma.

It's easier to become freed from offenses in Navadvīpa than in Vṛndāvana. It's mentioned that if there's any offenses that are committed in Vṛndāvana, then there is no way of eradicating the reactions to these offenses anywhere else in the world.

Since Navadvīpa and Vṛndāvana are on the same platform, it is advised that if someone commits offenses in Vṛndāvana, then he should resort to Navadvīpa in order to easily overcome the reactions to the offenses committed in Vṛndāvana. Therefore, those who are not actually very qualified in the matter of following the principles of devotional service, uttama-bhakti, they are advised that they should briefly visit Vṛndāvana and spend more time in Navadvīpa.

November 30, 2001

Two days ago, we spoke on the first paragraph of this purport. [Pūrṇacandra Prabhu reads]:

apy eṇa-patny upagataḥ priyayeha gātrais
tanvan dṛśāṁ sakhi su-nirvṛtim acyuto vaḥ
kāntāṅga-saṅga-kuca-kuṅkuma-rañjitāyāḥ
kunda-srajaḥ kula-pater iha vāti gandhaḥ
(Śrīmad-Bhāgavatam 10.30.11)

This is such a nice verse because it allows us – to some extent, to the extent of our ability – to get the scent of the beauty of Kṛṣṇa, the attraction of Kṛṣṇa, and the nature of Kṛṣṇa's influence upon the most highly elevated realized souls in the mādhurya, or conjugal, rasa.

"O friend, wife of the deer, has Lord Acyuta been here with His beloved, bringing great joy to your eyes? Indeed, blowing this way is the fragrance of His garland of kunda flowers, which was smeared with the kuṅkuma from the breast of His girlfriend when He embraced Her."

This is such a beautiful description. It creates a great thirst within our hearts to actually personally witness the nikuñja-līlās of Rādhā and Kṛṣṇa. Rādhārāṇī and Kṛṣṇa are the supreme emblem of conjugal loving affairs. If Rādhā and Kṛṣṇa were not absorbed in relishing conjugal love or conjugal affairs in Goloka-dhāma, there would be no question of any semblance or perverted reflection of the affair in this material world. Śrī Caitanya Mahāprabhu has mercifully revealed to us this most esoteric understanding of the truths of Godhead. It's important for us to understand that the living entity conditioned soul's endeavor to imitate God necessarily requires his indulgence in sex life. Mundane sex life between the apparent prakṛti and puruṣa manifestations of this world in the form of females and males, or women and men particularly, and any other female and male manifestation in any species of life, they are all the expression of the conditioned soul's desire to play God.

In fact, there are descriptions in the Śrīmad-Bhāgavatam – particularly in the Fifth Canto, in the chapter in which we find the descriptions of the subterranean heavenly planets, we will see that in these subterranean heavenly planets where there is basically more facility for material enjoyment even than in the heavenly planets, we will find that the women of that realm seduce the men for exploitative purposes because it's on a material platform, and when the men will conjugate with those women of that world, at their time of conjugation, they will actually be convinced that they are God. The men will be convinced that they have become God on account of their sexual experiences.

Bhū-maṇḍala is like a plateau which is dividing the upper worlds from the nether worlds. Since that realm is below Bhū-maṇḍala, the sunshine does not reach that section of the universe. Because the sunshine is not observable, because the course of the sun is not observable, there is no way of actually measuring the passage of time. The movement of the sun is not observable on account of the fact that it has been covered by the Bhū-maṇḍala.

On those planets – we are talking about the subterranean heavenly planets – there is no way of measuring the passage of time. It is described that the skies in those planets are illumined by the brilliant, self-effulgent jewels on the heads of the Nāgas, the serpents. The residents of that realm, they actually have the greatest facility for being in the illusion that they are eternally established. So it's quite possible for them to think that they are eternal enjoyers. They actually have the greatest facility for pretending to be God.

In this world – because the sun is rising and setting and we can easily detect the aging of our bodies, we can see the movement of time easily. But it is not so easy for us to conclude that we are not under some superior control, although in our ignorance, we may attempt to doggedly attach ourselves to that conception.

In any case, whether one is in the lower planetary systems, whether one is in the middle planetary systems or in the higher planetary systems, enjoying heavenly delights in Svargaloka, etc. – in any case, the activities of sex between male and female counterparts are an expression of the conditioned soul's desire to imitate Godhead.

As you must be knowing, Godhead is not complete without its constituents. Constituents means aspects or parts. In the Absolute Truth, there are both: energetic and energy. The energy and the energetic are simultaneously one and different from each other. We can understand that when there is an enjoyer, there must be an enjoyed. Without having something to enjoy, there is no meaning of being an enjoyer. Kṛṣṇa, as the supreme enjoyer, expands His very Self in the form of that which He is to enjoy. And in this way, Rādhā and Kṛṣṇa are simultaneously manifest in a differentiated way, although They are one. In the beginning, the Absolute Truth was one. It is described in Caitanya-caritāmṛta, in the beginning the Absolute Truth was all combined in one form as Śrī Kṛṣṇa. But to relish enhanced pleasure pastimes, He has divided Himself into two in the form of Rādhā and Kṛṣṇa. Rādhā is Kṛṣṇa. She is the enjoyed aspect of Kṛṣṇa.

You must be knowing that on the full-moon night of the śarat season, when Kṛṣṇa came to Vaṁśīvaṭa, Cupid, Kāmadeva, thought to attack Kṛṣṇa. Taking all his weapons with him, Kāmadeva approached rāsa-maṇḍala at Vaṁśīvaṭa in order to wage war against Kṛṣṇa. You will find this statement in Śrīmad-Bhāgavatam: yoga-māyām upāśritaḥ, which means that this rāsa-dancing is under the influence of Kṛṣṇa's yogamāyā. This rāsa-dancing is not like the dancing of the young boys and girls in this perverted world of material sense gratification, but rather it is under the influence of yogamāyā, completely on the spiritual platform. Mahāmāyā has no influence in these affairs. As such, there is no question of any inebriety or fault in the matter of Kṛṣṇa's association with the young housewives of Vraja.

Anyhow, yogamāyā served Kṛṣṇa by dressing Him so nicely that when Cupid approached Him with all of his best weapons, he became so bewildered, so enchanted in a bewildering way, and that is called mohana. Kāmadeva became so enchanted that he lost his senses and fell in a heap, unconscious on the ground of Vraja. Hence Kṛṣṇa, on account of His unparalleled unexcelled transcendental beauty and sweetness, is known as Madan-mohana, the enchanter, or the bewilderer, of Kāmadeva, Cupid. He appears as the new Kāmadeva with all His super-enchanting sweetness. This new Kāmadeva is represented in the Kāma-gāyatrī mantra.

Those who have received the pāñcarātrika-vaiṣṇava-dīkṣā in our line must be knowing the Kāma-gāyatrī mantra, and must be regularly doing this mantra-upāsanā. This mantra-upāsanā of the Kāma-gāyatrī mantra and the Gopāla mantra, eighteen-syllable Gopāla mantra as we have it, it is not an ordinary affair.

In Upadeśāmṛta, it is mentioned that there are six causes of the fall-down of a devotee. One of those causes is called niyamāgraha. Niyamāgraha means to attach oneself to the rules and regulations without understanding the purpose behind them, or to give up the regulative principles without understanding the purpose behind them. For us to become fixed up and to remain fixed up in our pursuit of the perfection of unalloyed kevala-bhakti, or devotional service, following in the footsteps of the residents of Vraja, it is very essential for us to understand the purpose behind the aspects of devotional practices that our spiritual masters have given us.

My speech at this point is a kind of ad-libbing – I didn't prepare anything particularly to say, so I am depending on Kṛṣṇa to provide the words to me circumstantially. If I had prepared, I would have brought with me Śrīpāda Dhyānacandra's paddhati in order to give full expression to the thing I want to put across.

Śrīpāda Dhyānacandra's paddhati is Gaura-govindārcana-smaraṇa-paddhati. In this book, Dhyānacandra Prabhu – just so that you may know the authority or the authoritative status of Dhyānacandra Prabhupāda, we can say that he is the illustrious disciple of Gopāla-guru Gosvāmī. Does anyone not know who is Gopāla-guru Gosvāmī? Gopāla-guru Gosvāmī was given the title of guru by Śrī Caitanya Mahāprabhu.

One time, Śrī Caitanya Mahāprabhu was going to do his ablutions. And as He was going to pass in His nara-līlā, He was holding His tongue because His tongue could not stop chanting Hare Kṛṣṇa. So He was holding His tongue to keep it from vibrating the Holy Name.

At that time, it so happened that one little boy, Gopāla, was watching Him, and when he saw Him holding His tongue, Gopāla asked Him, "What are you doing? Why are you holding your tongue?

This is a very strange thing, someone holding his tongue while he is …" So it was surprising Gopāla. Mahāprabhu explained to Gopāla, "Because I am passing, this a contaminated activity. I don't want that the Holy Name should enter into this contaminated atmosphere. I should not chant the Holy Name at such times when I am contaminating."

Then Gopāla said, "Āre bābā! What are you talking about? What are you doing? You are the Supreme Absolute Truth, eternally liberated. For You, there is no fault! And if You chant the Holy Name during the time of defecation or if You don't chant the Holy Name, it makes no difference ultimately because even your defecation is in itself transcendentally situated. But you should think for the benefit and welfare of the fallen conditioned souls of this world. What if they die at the time when they are passing stool? Then what recourse will they have for their deliverance? And besides, the Holy Name is pavitram uttamam. It is above and beyond. Just like the sun. The sun beats down on any contaminated place and purifies that contaminated place without becoming contaminated himself. The Holy Name cannot become contaminated by entering into a contaminated atmosphere. And besides, there is no rule of time and place and condition upon the chanting of the Holy Name. If You will set such an example of holding Your tongue and all the fallen conditioned souls will follow suit and hold their tongues, then if they die during the time when they pass stool, where is the question of their deliverance?"

At that point, Śrī Caitanya Mahāprabhu said, "Oh, oh, yes, yes! From now on, you will be called guru. You are my guru because you have instructed me quite rightly in this matter. I have heard the perfect conclusion from your lotus mouth."

From that day on, little Gopāla was known among the Vaiṣṇavas – even though he was a young lad – as

Gopāla-guru Gosvāmī. He became the illustrious disciple of Śrīpāda Vakreśvara Paṇḍita. Vakreśvara Paṇḍita was one of the only two dīkṣā disciples of Śrī Caitanya Mahāprabhu. The other one is said to be as Lokanātha Gosvāmī, who is the spiritual master or the dīkṣā guru of Narottama dāsa Ṭhākura.

Dhyānacandra is the disciple of that Gopāla-guru Gosvāmī, and he, under the instructions of Gopāla-guru Gosvāmī, had received instructions from Svarūpa Dāmodara Gosvāmī in the matter of compiling the system of rāga-bhajana which is called the bahiraṅgā aspect of rāgānuga-bhakti, or the external process or gradual course, the process by which one can gradually develop the inclination toward the rāga-bhajana.

Without going any further into that discussion, the purpose of all this is to point out the essence of what was instructed by Dhyānacandra in his paddhati concerning the purpose behind our chanting of the Kāma-gāyatrī mantra. The purpose of doing any devotional service is to attain the goal of the devotional service. The process is called abhidheya, and the goal is the attainment of our prime necessity, or prema-prayojana, prayojana-siddhi. So we should recognize what is our necessity, what is that prayojana. And what is our guru-varga or our guru family, our family of disciplic succession – what are they actually giving us?

Dhyānacandra Gosvāmī in his paddhati explains, with reference to the Purāṇas and various other Vaiṣṇava literatures, what is the goal of the chanting of Hare Kṛṣṇa mahā-mantra, what is the goal of the chanting of the ten-syllable and eighteen-syllable Gopāla mantra, and what is the goal of the chanting of the Kāma-gāyatrī mantra, the Rādhā mantra, the Rādhā-gāyatrī, the aṣṭa-sakhī mantras, and the aṣṭa-mañjarī mantras. All these things are described in Dhyānacandra's paddhati.

It's very essential for us to understand why we are doing what we are doing. It's not enough just to go through the motions just because we have been pushed to do something. What is the goal of our devotional activities?

Dhyānacandra, with reference to the śāstras, establishes that the goal of the chanting of the Hare Kṛṣṇa mantra – What is the result of chanting the Hare Kṛṣṇa mahā-mantra? The result of chanting the Hare Kṛṣṇa mahā-mantra is that you attain the land of Vraja.

That is applicable both in the stages of sādhana and in the stages of siddhi, or sādhya.

The siddhas, they will attain the land of Kṛṣṇa's Bhauma-vṛndāvana during the time when Kṛṣṇa's pastimes will be enacted in a particular universe.

And the sādhakas, by chanting the Hare Kṛṣṇa mantra, will attain this Vraja-bhūmi by the grace of the chanting of the Hare Kṛṣṇa mahā-mantra.

You may understand now how it is that all of us have been graced by the attainment of the blessing of being able to put our two feet upon the dust of this land of Vraja-bhūmi. It is by the grace of our association with this Hare Kṛṣṇa mahā-mantra which has been propagated all over the world by Śrīla Prabhupāda and the followers of Śrīla Prabhupāda.

According to Dhyānacandra's paddhati it should be concluded that the purpose of our propagating the chanting of the Hare Kṛṣṇa mahā-mantra all over the world is to broadcast the glories of Rādhā and Kṛṣṇa, and to attract living entities to this realm of Vraja-bhūmi, and to ultimately facilitate their attainment of the transcendental spiritual forms with which to play with Kṛṣṇa, to dance with Kṛṣṇa, and to go back home, back to Godhead, back to Goloka-vraja-dhāma, or to the aprākṛta-līlās of Kṛṣṇa. That is the only purpose for our propagation of the Hare Kṛṣṇa mahā-mantra. There is no other purpose. If we are thinking that there is any other purpose, then in reality, we are not closely adhering to the principles of our Gauḍīya ācāryas. The result of which is that we will get something of a different order.

Similarly, Dhyānacandra points out that the chanting of the eighteen- and ten-syllable Gopāla mantra – What is the result of chanting these mantras? The result is that you will attain the darśana of Vrajendra-nandana Gopāla. By the chanting of this mantra, it is not to be expected that we will attain the darśana of Dvārakādīśa or that we will attain the darśana of Rāmacandra or Nārāyaṇa. If we do by some chance – as the sages of Daṇḍakāraṇya got the darśana of Rāmacandra or if we – like the gopīs by chance got the darśana of the four-armed form of the Lord, then with all humility at our command, we will beg at Their lotus feet, meaning Rāmacandra's lotus feet or the four-armed Lord's lotus feet, to please show us our iṣṭa-devatā, the most beautiful, the sweetest of all sweetnesses, the unlimitedly honey-moon-faced Vrajendra-nandana Gopāla! Kṛṣṇa has a honey-moon face. Have you never seen? Honey-moon face ... Anyway, don't try to see Kṛṣṇa. Try to act in such a way that Kṛṣṇa wants to see you.

Furthermore, Dhyānacandra describes that the result, or the goal, of chanting the eighteen-syllable Gopāla mantra is that we get the darśana of Vrajendra-nandana Gopāla. If we chant attentively, purely, with the desire to attain Him, then that mantra will fulfill our desires. That we have already discussed. But the result of chanting the twenty-four-and-a-half-syllable Kāma-gāyatrī mantra is that you attain the prema-sevās at the lotus feet of Rādhā and Kṛṣṇa.

Also, it is described what is the result of chanting the Rādhā mantra. The Rādhā mantra is chanted by the pūjārīs who are worshiping Rādhārāṇī. They are given access to chant the Rādhā mantra on account of them having been initiated into the king of all mantras, the Kāma-gāyatrī, and they also have rights to chant other mantras which will be as corollaries of that mantra. By chanting the Rādhā mantra, one attains exclusive devotion at the lotus feet of Rādhā. And by chanting the Lalitā mantra, one gets prema for Rādhā and Kṛṣṇa from the standpoint of the sakhī. By chanting the Viśākhā mantra, one will augment, or enhance, that prema. And similarly, there are results of chanting the other aṣṭa-sakhī mantras; the result of chanting the aṣṭa-mañjarī mantras is that you'll attain the realm of Vraja.

As well, there is a discussion on the chanting of the Gaura mantra. It's described that the Gaura mantra can be chanted beginning with the bīja mantra srīṁ, hrīṁ, aiṁ, and klīṁ. It mentions that if the Gaura mantra will be combined with the bīja mantra klīṁ which is the kāma-bīja, then that Gaura mantra will fulfill all desires. Kṛṣṇa, as we have been discussing, is the transcendental Kāmadeva. Kāma means desires. Kṛṣṇa is the mādhurya-svarūpa of that Kāmadeva. And Gaura is the audārya-svarūpa of the very same Kāmadeva. When we have a desire, that desire is like a prayer to the lotus feet of Kṛṣṇa.

[Sings]: A house and a car and a color TV, jaya jagadīśa hari! If you have a desire, that is a prayer to Kṛṣṇa. And Kṛṣṇa is so kind to us that He makes varieties of arrangements for the fulfillment of our various desires. If we desire to eat like a hog or have sex like a hog, or a dog:

ṛṣabha uvāca
nāyaṁ deho deha-bhājāṁ nṛloke
kaṣṭān kāmān arhate viḍ-bhujāṁ ye
tapo divyaṁ putrakā yena sattvaṁ
śuddhyed yasmād brahma-saukhyaṁ tv anantam
(Śrīmad-Bhāgavatam 5.5.1)

Lord Ṛṣabhadeva is telling that we should not involve ourselves with the pursuit of so-called happinesses or so-called pleasures which are enjoyed by the hogs and dogs which eat stool. No, we should not desire those things, but rather we should desire, on the basis of the desire for a higher platform of experience in loving devotional service, we should perform tapo divyaṁ, tapo divyaṁ putrakā yena sattvaṁ śuddhyed yasmād brahma-saukhyaṁ tv anantam to get spiritual happiness which is eternal, unlimited. In other words, what Lord Ṛṣabhadeva is telling us in short is, "Why allow yourself to be confined to the very paltry, pale, stale, putrid activities of mundane sense-gratification when you can have something of such a higher order which will give you an experience which will actually satisfy your ānanda-mayo 'bhyāsāt nature as an eternal living entity, an eternal servant of Kṛṣṇa?"

Śrīla Prabhupāda has instructed us that Vṛndāvana and Kṛṣṇa are non-different. Just like Kṛṣṇa as Kāmadeva, He fulfills all desires, so similarly, Vṛndāvana-dhāma is like a desire tree which fulfills all desires. But he has warned us that we should be very careful what we desire when we are in Vṛndāvana-dhāma, because those desires will be fulfilled, but maybe not in a way that you'll expect them to be fulfilled. Therefore we should be very careful. If we desire bhukti, then Kṛṣṇa will give us bhukti. Bhukti means material sense gratification. Like the hogs and dogs.

One time, there was one brāhmaṇa who was lusting after a prostitute. I'll try to shorten the story: His wife went to serve that prostitute in order to invoke her mercy and as remuneration for her services, she requested that the prostitute should consort with her husband. When the arrangement was made that the brāhmaṇa went to the prostitute's house – as you know, the way to a man's heart is through his stomach – the prostitute had made the arrangements for a nice repast, or meal, before the spectacular event.

When the brāhmaṇa was seated nicely for taking his meal, he was surprised: "What is this?!" Here was a clay pot with porridge in it, and here was an iron pot with porridge in it, and here was a silver pot with porridge in it, a gold pot with porridge in it, and a diamond pot with porridge in it.

Upon his inquiry, the prostitute explained to him, "You are thinking that just because it's in a diamond pot or a gold pot or a silver pot or an iron pot or a clay pot, there is some difference. But actually, the taste is the same. So similarly, sex life in any species of life basically has the same disgusting, abominable feature which is only overlooked by those who are blinded by lust."

In this way, she instructed and he came to his senses and returned to his wife unblemished. In any case, we should be very careful what we desire when we come to Vṛndāvana-dhāma. Vṛndāvana-dhāma is mādhurya-dhāma, and it is meant for augmenting our consciousness with the beauty of Kṛṣṇa and Rādhārāṇī's mādhurya-līlās. There is really no other purpose to be fulfilled in coming to Vṛndāvana-dhāma than to increase, or enhance, our appreciation of the beauty of those līlās.

Kṛṣṇa is very strict! He is not so lenient in the matter of His reciprocation with the devotees. Prabhupāda had instructed that in the worship of Gaura-Nitāi – because Gaura-Nitāi are the audārya feature of Kṛṣṇa-Balarāma, taking the humble position being munificent – They consider no offenses in Their worship.

Jagannātha, Baladeva, and Subhadrā consider 50 percent of the offenses in Their worship. But Rādhā and Kṛṣṇa, although They are very kind and benevolent and merciful, still They express Their mercy in a particular way, in a certain way as to put pressure on the devotees to upgrade their consciousness by considering 75 percent of the offenses in Their worship. That is why in Vṛndāvana-dhāma, the offenses are magnified, the reactions to the offenses committed here are magnified a thousand-fold.

However, in Gaura-dhāma, in Navadvīpa-dhāma, the offenses are not multiplied or magnified a thousand-fold. However, as we see in the case of Jagāi and Mādhāi offending Lord Nityānanda, and also Gopāla Cāpāla's offense at the feet of Śrīvāsa Ṭhākura when he put the wine pots and various paraphernalia for Kālī-pūjā at his doorstep to defame him, these offenses against the Vaiṣṇavas are not easily overlooked by Śrī Caitanya Mahāprabhu.

However, just like the name of Kṛṣṇa is more merciful than Kṛṣṇa Himself, so similarly the name of Gaura is more merciful than Gaura Himself. Simply by once chanting the name "Śrī Kṛṣṇa Caitanya," one is freed from the reactions to all offenses.

kṛṣṇa-caitanya-nāmnā ye kīrtayanti sakṛn naraḥ
nanaparādha-muktas te punanti sakalaṁ jagat

And if you chant the name Śrī Kṛṣṇa Caitanya in Vṛndāvana-dhāma, you'll get a thousand times, a million times, the benefit. Prabhupāda advised us, especially as bungling neophytes, to take shelter of the names of Gaura by chanting the Pañca-tattva mahā-mantra: "Śrī Kṛṣṇa Caitanya, Prabhu Nityānanda, Śrī Advaita, Gadādhara, Śrīvāsa-ādi gaura-bhakta-vṛnda." And then chant, "Hare Kṛṣṇa, Hare Kṛṣṇa, Kṛṣṇa Kṛṣṇa, Hare Hare / Hare Rāma, Hare Rāma, Rāma Rāma, Hare Hare."

The process of properly performing kīrtana as described by our ācāryas is that first you do Guru-vandanām. First we perform guru-kīrtana, and invoking the mercy of guru, with his benign, merciful benediction, we approach the lotus feet of Lord Gaura and His associates by doing gaura-kīrtana. Then by the grace of Gaura-nāma, we will more or less wipe our slate clean. We'll clean our slate, or we'll have chance to turn over a new leaf every time we attempt to chant the Holy Names of Kṛṣṇa in the kṛṣṇa-kīrtana.

Just like Citragupta is writing down all the virtues and faults of a living entity in his book of life as the secretary of Yamarāja, so similarly we should not think that the offenses that we commit against the Holy Name are not being tabulated. If you want to advance in Kṛṣṇa consciousness, if you want to attain the realm of Vraja, if you have even a glimmer of hope in your heart to see the pastimes of Rādhā and Kṛṣṇa and the gopīs and cowherd boys, then you must absolutely essentially take shelter of the name of Śrī Caitanya Mahāprabhu.

If you will understand this principle, ardently attach

yourself to the chanting of the Gaura mantra, beginning with the kāma-bīja mantra that is klīṁ. Klīṁ gaurāya, etc. If you will attach yourself to this chanting of the Gaura mantra, then that Gaura mantra will fulfill all your desires. If you commit any offense in the matter of approaching the transcendental subject matter of Kṛṣṇa and Kṛṣṇa's devotional service and the ultimate realization or the purpose of devotional service in the matter of attainment of the service to the līlās of Kṛṣṇa, then by committing any offense in this regard will certainly make it virtually impossible for us to attain our desired goal in this lifetime,.

However, if our purpose is set up in spite of all of our faults, if we take shelter of the names of Caitanya Mahāprabhu, then it will be much easier for us to overcome our anarthas by the execution of Rādhā- and Kṛṣṇa-bhajana. But the desire for progress in Kṛṣṇa consciousness should be there. Otherwise, it may be possible if we are so much attached to material sense gratification that Gaura will also allow us to continue with our nonsense. We should at least be on the clearing stage or attempting to clear away our offenses, to clear away our anarthas by taking shelter of the names of Lord Caitanya.

One other interesting point in this regard—if you don't mind, I would like to discuss a little more about the chanting of the Hare Kṛṣṇa mahā-mantra, because this is also a very useful understanding to be applied for our rapid progress to the chanting of the pure name. In that same Caitanya-candrāmṛta, it is told that Kṛṣṇa is very difficult to attain. Kṛṣṇa demands surrender first. Then if He sees that surrendered disposition in the course of an individual's devotional practices, He may condescend to give Himself to the devotee. Kṛṣṇa does not give Himself very easily. Similarly, Kṛṣṇa-nāma also does not give Himself very easily. Not all that comes from our mouth that is having the alphabetical configuration of K-R-S-N-A, Kṛṣṇa, is nāma. Even though it looks like nāma and sounds like nāma, it may be a māyic or external bahiraṅgā representation of nāma.

Just like during Kṛṣṇa's mauṣala-līlā in Dvārakā, Kṛṣṇa, when He was shot in the heel by a hunter, left a virāṭ-rūpa to bewilder the atheistic class of men. That virāṭ-rūpa looked exactly like Kṛṣṇa. That's how He was able to bewilder the atheistic class of men. If it didn't look like Kṛṣṇa, then they would easily be able to conclude that Kṛṣṇa had gone and here was something else, other than Kṛṣṇa. Similarly, Śrīla Bhaktisiddhānta comments on this subject matter that when Rāvaṇa took Sītā-devī, that Sītā-devī that he took looked exactly like Sītā-devī, and Rāvaṇa had the understanding that he had actually abducted Sītā-devī, that he had Sītā-devī in his grip.

But in fact, as it is disclosed by Caitanya Mahāprabhu to one crying brāhmaṇa on his way to South India – the brāhmaṇa was crying because he was distressed upon Rāvaṇa's abducting Sītā-devī. So on His South Indian tour, Caitanya Mahāprabhu gathered some evidence from śāstras that proved that Rāvaṇa had not in fact abducted Sītā-devī. When He came back from His South Indian tour, He was telling to that crying brāhmaṇa – he was still crying – and solidly proved to him from śāstra that Rāvaṇa had in fact not caught hold of Sītā-devī but had caught hold of a māyic form of Sītā.

Bhaktisiddhānta Sarasvatī Ṭhākura Prabhupāda instructs that sinful people and offenders against the Holy Name cannot in any way at any time chant the Holy Name of Kṛṣṇa.

nāhaṁ prakāśaḥ sarvasya
yoga-māyā-samāvṛtaḥ
mūḍho ,yaṁ nābhijānāti
loko mām ajam avyayam
(Bhagavad-gītā 7.25)

It's described in this verse that Kṛṣṇa covers Himself from the mūḍhas, from the fools and rascals and sinful offenders, by the curtain of yogamāyā. Kṛṣṇa reserves the right to be had or not to be had. He doesn't have to reveal Himself just because someone claps his hands, that we should expect that He will dance on our stage according to our tune.

It should be understood that even though a sinful or an offensive person may be appearing to chant, it is nāma apparently; it is not nāma in reality. It is a māyic sound vibration, and it is quite mundane, or material. And the result of associating with that sound vibration chanted by a non-devotee is that one becomes invested with material desires in the same way that milk when touched by the serpent has poisonous effects. It may look like milk, but in fact it is poison.

The pure name appears only in the heart of a devotee and dances on his or her tongue after the stage of anartha-nivṛtti. When Kṛṣṇa will be seeing the firm niṣṭhā, niṣṭhatā-bhajana, the firmly determined bhajana or attempts to worship the Holy Name, when He will see that an aspirant in the matter of the practice of chanting of the Holy Name is firmly determined in his nāma-bhajana and doesn't waver in his endeavors to propitiate or to beg the mercy of experiencing the divine appearance and transcendental association of Harināma Prabhu in his heart of hearts, then Kṛṣṇa, being attracted by that determined effort, by steady devotional attitude of the sādhaka may, or even may not agree – but He may descend from Goloka-dhāma, golokera prema-dhana, hari-nāma-saṅkīrtana. From Goloka-dhāma – Kṛṣṇa-nāma descends to the heart of that sādhaka, keeps that sādhaka company.

The offended name is devoid of antaraṅga-śakti, or the internal potencies of Kṛṣṇa – spiritual potencies. Aparādha-nāma is a manifestation of the bahiraṅgā-śakti or material potency, external potency. But śuddha-nāma is Kṛṣṇa Himself. There is aparādha-nāma, ābhāsa-nāma, which is like the tejas of Kṛṣṇa, or the paraṁ jyoti – how much ānanda can you expect to get from effulgence? How much enlightenment can you hope to have by associating with the Brahman effulgence? It is only when the divine sun of Kṛṣṇa-nāma chooses to arise within the sky of the heart that He appears along with all his spiritual śaktis, antaraṅga-śaktis to ignite the fire of prema which is dormant within the heart of every jīva.

Only at the time when the śuddha-nāma will make His divine descent to the heart of a pure devotee will he have the eligibility to initiate disciples into the chanting of the pure name. Anything done before that time is, you can say, more or less show bottle. It may be a lucrative venture, but it will not yield the desired effect in the matter of augmenting the prema-saṅkīrtana movement, in the matter of facilitating in oneself or in others the experience of this ānandāmbudhi-vardhanam aspect of the saṅkīrtana.

The point that I am trying to bring out – because if you remember, we were talking about Caitanya-candrāmṛta. Excuse me if our elaborations tend to diverge from the point, but I feel that it is necessary. If you can follow closely, just try to catch the ideas, and the elaboration will help to support and fill in the missing pieces of the puzzle.

The bottom line is that Kṛṣṇa and Kṛṣṇa's name, although They are merciful, are not so merciful. They don't give Themselves so easily. Kṛṣṇa demands surrender. Only on the basis of steady surrendered devotional attitude is He even prepared to consider giving Himself to any devotee. But Prabodhānanda Sarasvatīpāda tells in this śloka that, however, Lord Caitanya is so merciful that He is prepared to give Himself even to the non-devotee. What could that possibly mean, "non-devotee"? The question may arise that if we are not chanting the pure name of Kṛṣṇa, are we really devotees? Can anyone who is not having the privilege of having the divine association of the pure name seated on the lotus of the heart and dancing on our tongue, call himself a devotee? Can we even consider such a thing? If I think that I am a Vaiṣṇava, then I will look forward with the expectation of receiving honor from others and thus be engulfed in false pride. I will be enveloped or crushed by the jaws of false pride. And then surely I will go to hell. We cannot consider ourselves Vaiṣṇavas or devotees unless we are chanting the pure name of Kṛṣṇa.

That pure name of Kṛṣṇa is said to be recognizably manifest in the heart and in the life and in the words of a devotee, when the devotee is having profound ruci for devotional practices. In reality, the vast majority of the devotees in the movement, although they are fortunate to come to the feet of Śrīla Prabhupāda, although they are fortunate to have the association of others who may be chanting the pure name, still if we are not chanting the pure name, we should consider ourselves to be counted among the class of non-devotees.

It is not that by wearing the Vaiṣṇava tilaka and kaṇṭhī-mālā and keeping a śikhā or keeping a dhotī or a sari or any of these things, what to speak of punjabi dresses or shorts, that we can call them all as Vaiṣṇavas. Vaiṣṇava is a very high thing. Even a sādhaka may be regarded as a Vaiṣṇava; he is also sādhu if he is ardently attached to the service of sattam, satyam – truth! If he is an essence-seeking devotee, then he or she may be considered as a sādhu.

But if he or she is a mūḍha-like or ass-like devotee, who is characterized by the carrying around on his shoulder, on his head, on the other shoulder, on the back, his load of the various types of anarthas, then he can hardly be considered as a sadhu, because he is still attached to the mundane.

He may be in the fold of devotees, but he or she may not be considered, or consider oneself, as a devotee. If we are intelligent and if we can understand this about our fallen condition, as Bhaktisiddhānta Sarasvatī Ṭhākura instructs, anyone who is not chanting a minimum of sixty-four rounds daily is considered patita. So we should truly understand our fallen condition. That much su-medhasa [brain substance] we should be having.

And if we have that much su-medhasa to understand that we are counted among the patita, that perhaps we are not chanting the pure name, perhaps we are chanting nāma-ābhāsa, perhaps we are chanting aparādha-nāma, perhaps we are so fallen that we are not able to even make a very significant effort in the matter of even trying to come to the position of chanting the pure name. Bhaktivinoda Ṭhākura says that the madhyama-adhikārī chants a minimum of 192 rounds daily. 192 rounds daily! A madhyama-adhikārī! This is discussed by him in Śrī Caitanya-śikṣāmṛta, one of his books.

He says that the madhyama-adhikārī chants a minimum of three lakhs nāma daily. And why is he doing that? It is because that is the mark of his desire to cry out for the mercy of nāma. And that is because obviously no one could do that if he wasn't chanting the pure name. Because it is only when the pure name appears that Kṛṣṇa has actually appeared. Kṛṣṇa is raso vai saḥ, He is akhila-rasāmṛta-sindhu-mūrti, He is the embodiment of all rasa, and He is the source of relishment of all rasas. Since He is raso vai saḥ, we can understand that His appearance creates the tastefulness within our chanting.

In the māyic manifestation, there is not much to be tasted. We may be thinking that we are chanting and tasting something, but in truth we are tasting our ardent attachments to lobha, puja, and pratiṣṭhā, as well as various other mundane gratifications that may be awarded to us by the grace of the offended name. We could hardly think to get much taste from associating with the brahman-tejas of nāma.

That's why people who are chanting the offended name or people who are chanting on the clearing stage on the ābhāsa-nāma platform, that's why they struggle and struggle and struggle, because they are not having anything to taste, because Kṛṣṇa has not come there. Kṛṣṇa is tasteful! So when Kṛṣṇa comes, then He creates taste. He gives us the taste of Himself.

You can hardly think to get taste from something which is relatively tasteless. Only Kṛṣṇa and Kṛṣṇa-nāma is tasteful. When we say ruci, the state of ruci, or having profound ruci for pure devotional practices – because pure devotional service and Kṛṣṇa are non-different – we should understand that if one is having ruci, then only can it be seen that pure devotional service is being done and that the pure name is being chanted. But one has to be careful to discern whether or not we are actually having ruci, because there are also mundane perverted reflections of ruci.

There is the ābhāsa feature of ruci, and there is the ābhāsa feature of rati. That is in the form of chāyā-rati-ābhāsa, which is a shadow of ecstatic emotions which should be experienced by associating with exalted bhāvukas, or bhāva-bhaktas, or prema-bhaktas, premika-bhaktas. Or the pratibimba-rati-ābhāsa, which is experienced when one superimposes material concepts on the activities of devotion. If one becomes elated into thinking that, "By chanting the Holy Name, I will increase my bank balance, or if by making disciples I will increase my false prestige, or if I present myself as a Vaiṣṇava, as a guru of Vaiṣṇavas, that I will be adored by the neophyte classes of starry-eyed bhaktas," then we should understand that the taste which is arising from that may not be real ruci. Maybe something quite of a different order. We have to be careful to consider what taste we are attaching ourselves to.

Those who actually have ruci, the pure name, are characterized by the feasible na dhanaṁ, na janaṁ, na sundarīṁ, na mokṣam. I don't want to increase my wealth, my bank balance; I am not interested in this profit calculation for sense gratification; I am not concerned with maintaining my status quo in the matter of material comforts.

Even as devotees or aspiring devotees or somehow or other impostor devotees as it may be in various ways, we may attach ourselves to these lower forms of ruci. Just like it's described that in the matter of pure devotional service, or taste for pure devotional service, there are two kinds of ruci. One is a ruci which is derived from the association with Kṛṣṇa Himself. And another ruci, the lower order of ruci, which may be governed by the quality of the opulences surrounding Kṛṣṇa.

If the name is chanted with nice musical accompaniment, with nice rāga-alaṅkāras, etc., then, "Oh, this is a very nice kīrtana!" So sometimes to benefit persons who are of that status of pre-devotional predilection, we have to present kīrtana in such a nice way. It is like candy-coating the medicine, so to speak. Our real intention is to give them a chance to associate with the chanting of the pure name. Similarly, someone may take pleasure in worshiping the Deity only if there is nice silver paraphernalia, nice dresses and ornaments, and especially nice mahā-prasāda! Anyway, previously we discussed how to honor the mahā-prasāda and the pitfalls of applying mundane consciousness to our so-called relishment of mahā-prasāda. No need to further elaborate on this point.

What we mean to say is that Caitanya Mahāprabhu is so kind that He is prepared to give Himself even to the non-devotees like us. That statement is to give us great hope. If we take this information and apply it to the discussion on the distinction between Kṛṣṇa-nāma and Gaura-nāma, we can enter into a tattva which is very, very, very, very sanguine and important to understand about the chanting of the Hare Kṛṣṇa mahā-mantra and which will help anyone who is not yet chanting the pure name to quickly come to the platform of chanting pure Kṛṣṇa-nāma. At least more quickly – compared to what?

Śrīla Prabhupāda's Teachings of Lord Caitanya

has been translated into Russian language; you can certainly refer to this and see for yourself what I am talking about. Because many times, for those who are less astute or who read less deeply, many statements may go unnoticed. But here is a very, very beautiful statement by Śrīla Prabhupāda which should be noted very carefully.

If I recall correctly, the same statement is repeated in both – in the introduction of Teachings of Lord Caitanya and also in the introduction to Śrī Caitanya-caritāmṛta. You may not have heard these things before, so it may sound surprising to you or it may sound different to you if you have not heard these things before or if you have not noticed these things in Śrīla Prabhupāda's teachings, but with a sober mind and intelligently, we should try to see the value of the forthcoming statements.

Śrīla Prabhupāda states, "In the Hare Kṛṣṇa mahā-mantra, you will see that there is the name of Kṛṣṇa and the name of Rāma."

I am paraphrasing and purporting a little bit also as we go along because that is my nature, but I'll try to give a synopsis. The idea he is giving is that Brajendra-nandana jei, śacī-suta hoilo sei, balarāma hoilo nitāi. Brajendra-nandana jei, śacī-suta hoilo sei – that the one who was previously Vrajendra-nandana, He has appeared as Śacī-suta, Śrī Caitanya Mahāprabhu. And who was previously Balarāma, He has appeared as Lord Nityānanda. This is from the introduction. We are just reading this point from Prabhupāda's introduction. Prabhupāda is saying, "Therefore in the Hare Kṛṣṇa mahā-mantra, the name Kṛṣṇa may be understood to denote Gaura," Śacī-suta, and the name Rāma, Hare Rāma, Hare Rāma, Rāma Rāma, Hare Hare. This name Rāma – because it also means Balarāma, Rāma means Rāmacandra, Rāma means Balarāma, Rāma means Rādhikā-ramaṇa, Paraśu-rāma. Rāma can mean any Rāma. It can also mean Rād-hā; for those who are tuned in a little to those things, they can mean Rādhā.

But for the purpose of presenting this understan-ding, Prabhupāda chooses to accept that at least in this case, in the case of this discussion, Rāma shall mean Balarāma. As Rāma has re-appeared in the form of Nitāi, whom we discussed previously as being combined with His svarūpa-śakti manifestations. Just like Mahāprabhu was combined with His svarūpa-śakti manifestations as Rādhā, Lalitā, and various others, so Rāma, Balarā-ma combined with his svarūpa-śakti manifestations as Anaṅga-mañjarī, as Revatī, as Vāruṇī and various gopa manifestations as well, they are all included within the transcendental form of Nityānanda, thus enabling Bala-rāma to relish the rasas which He was unable to relish in his previous līlā in the Kṛṣṇa-pīṭha.

Balarāma has appeared as Nitāi, and Nitāi is to be taken as non-different from the name of Rāma in the Hare Kṛṣṇa mahā-mantra, Nityānanda-Rāma. Nityānan-da-Rāma and Nityānanda-Rāma-nāma has the audārya aspect punctuated with the transcendental eligibility to relish the mādhurya-rasa on account of the presence of Anaṅga-mañjarī within Him. That Rāma-nāma in the mahā-mantra is fully capable of manifesting the audārya aspect of Rāma-nāma in the matter of facilitating the services of Gaura in the pursuit of Rādhā and Kṛṣṇa-bhajana.

It's probably not so complicated. I am not purposely trying to make it sound complicated so as to show myself to be so highly intelligent. Rather, my complex expressions indicate my lack of intelligence in the matter of simplifying things, so I am pretending.

Within all this discussion lies a very beautiful zenith that if in the course of your Hare Kṛṣṇa mahā-mantra-bhajana, if you will concentrate on the chanting of Holy Name of Kṛṣṇa, Hare Kṛṣṇa, denoting Gaura, and because Gaura-nāma is even more merciful then Gaura Himself, and Gaura Himself is the audārya-svarūpa of Kṛṣṇa, Kṛṣṇa is the mādhurya-svarūpa of Gaura and Gaura is the audārya-svarūpa of Kṛṣṇa.

Audārya means magnanimous, that Gaura Himself is prepared to give Himself even to the non-devotees likes us. So how much more we should expect – because Gaura-nāma is more merciful than Gaura, Nityānanda-nāma is more merciful than Nitāi. How much more we should expect that Gaura-nāma and Nityānanda-nāma, who are absolutely pure, who don't consider any offenses, who rather completely obliterate all reactions to all offenses, how much are we to hope that Gaura-nāma and Nityānanda-nāma in the form of Hare Kṛṣṇa and Hare Rāma will be inclined to give Themselves to us?

So Prabhupāda is telling that in the Hare Kṛṣṇa mahā-mantra, the name Kṛṣṇa can denote Gaura, and the name Rāma can denote Nitāi. That little information which he gives should lead us to draw out a conclusion: Gadāi Gaurāṅga, Gadāi Gaurāṅga, Gaurāṅga Gaurāṅga, Gadāi Gadāi – Jāhnavā Nitāi, Jāhnavā Nitāi, Nitāi Nitāi, Jāhnavā Jāhnavā – by chanting the mahā-mantra with this understanding, then our chanting of the mahā-mantra will very quickly manifest the pure name of the audārya feature of mādhurya-līlā-mayī-Kṛṣṇa. Heno nitāi bine bhāi, rādhā-kṛṣṇa pāite nāi [first śloka from Nityānanda Niṣṭha, by Narottama dāsa Ṭhākura]. You will read a very interesting statement in Caitanya-bhāgavata by Vṛndāvana dāsa Ṭhākura that it is only by the mercy of Lord Nityānanda that devotional service, following in the footsteps of the vraja-gopīs in the mood of rādhā-dāsyam or mañjarī-bhāva, has been spread all over the world. And implied in that statement is also Jāhnavā because at that time, Nityānanda had married to Jāhnavā and Vasudhā Mātā when he went back to Bengal for his preaching under the order of Lord Caitanya.

Therefore, I strongly recommend on the basis of my own personal experience that when you chant the Hare Kṛṣṇa mahā-mantra, at least 50 percent of your japa should be chanted taking full shelter at the lotus feet of Lord Nityānanda if you want the mercy of the damsels of Vraja. [Back to the reading from Śrīmad-Bhāgavatam 10.30.11]

"Kṛṣṇa had given up the company of all the other gopīs in order to sport with Me alone, and then He eventually renounced Me also. Please listen to the truth about why He did this. Vrajendra-nandana Kṛṣṇa is the ocean of love, and yet He neglects all other girls in My favor." Who is speaking? Rādhārāṇī is speaking.

So we are now going to hear an exhibition of Rādhārāṇī's understanding of the principles of pure love for Kṛṣṇa, which should help us to understand something about the moods of Vraja, which should help us to get a foothold in our appreciation of our real purpose in coming here.

"Vrajendra-nandana Kṛṣṇa is the ocean of love, and yet He neglects all other girls in My favor. But this behavior is not a fault of His, and here is the reason for this. He had seated Me on the lion-throne of matchless divine jewels of great fortune and personally decorated Me with the ornaments of many sportive amorous pastimes, shared as We wandered from forest to forest, making love. He enacted all this without even once remembering any other gopī."

In this sentence, Śrīmatī Rādhārāṇī expresses Kṛṣṇa's ardent exclusive attachment to Her. But because He is exclusively attached to Her, just see what happens. Rādhārāṇī continues, "But then I began to ponder over the situation." Ponder means to consider.

Because remember, Kṛṣṇa had called all the gopīs, as we have been reading about in Śrīmad-Bhāgavatam, and in so many ways, He was flirting with them, presenting apparently discouraging arguments, and at long last was defeated by the gopīs' arguments, at which point He agreed to accept them and began to sport with them in various ways, at which time the gopīs began to think themselves to be the most fortunate girls in all the universe and in certain respects began to nourish an egocentric conception of their relationship with Kṛṣṇa, at which time Kṛṣṇa thought to show mercy upon them by bringing them under the shelter of Rādhā's lotus feet, which could only be accomplished if He were to show the supremacy of Rādhā's love for Him.

Then He disappeared along with Rādhārāṇī, and as we have been reading, all the other gopīs are searching for Kṛṣṇa with the expectation of somehow or other attaining Him. They are wandering from bush to bush, from tree to tree, and begging the Mother Earth and here in our present verse, they are begging the deer, hoping that the deer will – due to their natural affection for Kṛṣṇa – bring them to the lotus feet of Kṛṣṇa.

Here is Kṛṣṇa with Rādhārāṇī, and Kṛṣṇa is enjoying exclusively with Rādhārāṇī, not even considering the various qualifications of the various other girls who are all unlimitedly more qualified than any woman of this world. But Rādhārāṇī is karuṇa-mayī; She is very merciful to Her devotees and very merciful to all the residents of Vraja. And because She is very kind-hearted, She wants to make arrangements for others to also meet with Kṛṣṇa. Here She is saying that, "I began to ponder over the situation. My dear girlfriends have not been enjoying the great festival of this fathomless ocean of ecstatic nectar but instead are burning miserably in feeling our separation. Why must this be and what can I do about it?"

See, She is feeling for Her girlfriends like that. She is not selfishly attached to Kṛṣṇa. It's not exactly like this, but sometimes if you have something very nice, you want to share it with someone else, and by sharing it with someone else, you'll experience an expansion of your appreciation of the thing.

Also, in the material world you have the pride of being the provider of the wonderful commodity to your friend or whoever. So we can also allow that to manifest, or not allow, but understand that it has its origin in the transcendental world in its pure feature.

Pūrṇacandra Prabhu: You just said that the gopīs or the sakhīs, her friends are burning in a – what is called – a fathomless ocean of feelings of separation. In this verse, they are using the word kula-pati, they are calling Kṛṣṇa kula-pati. So kula means a group of gopīs, and pati means Lord. So they are calling Him like that because they are feeling it's a right injustice that He is the Lord of all of us, but now He has gone away with only one. This is unfair! What an injustice. He should be here with us! Why He went away with one girl?

And therefore, then they called Him Acyuta, and acyuta means infallible, but it also gives the sense that He will never be lost. So they address Kṛṣṇa as Acyuta while they are talking to the doe and saying that, "You must know where He is! He is never acyuta to you, acyuta, He is never lost to you! Because we can see by the gleam in your eyes that you must have seen Him. Please tell us so that we can join Him." These are mentioned by Viśvanātha Cakravartī Ṭhākura.

Aindra Prabhu: So?

Pūrṇacandra Prabhu: Because you said that Śrīmatī Rādhārāṇī is mentioning that her friends are feeling separation and that they are expressing that in this verse.

Aindra Prabhu: There is another entry that could be added here. Rādhārāṇī is quite aware that just as in the material word, every woman has a concept or a vanity of her own beauty and qualifications on the platform of lust, just like love is blind or lust is blind, and because in the material world we have a tendency to absorb our consciousness in an extended selfish sense gratification, so we have a tendency to think, "I am best!" "My community is best!" "My country is best" and these types of vanities which may arise.

On the material platform, generally it is seen that the vanity that a woman will be having in the matter of her own beauty will be based or centered around the purposeful use of that beauty in the matter of exploiting others for her personal sense gratification in some way or another. But on the spiritual platform, the transcendental women, they also have what appears to be a similar type of vanity, but it should be understood that it is based on a preoccupation with the desire to employ their personal bodily beauty and various qualifications and artistry for the pleasure of Kṛṣṇa. Just like in the chapter of Kṛṣṇa book where it is describing the gopīs' feelings of separation – in that chapter, it is mentioned that when Kṛṣṇa was walking with His beloveds through the forest, He would touch the leaves and fruits and branches and flowers of the various trees creepers, giving them great joy.

This section is purported by saying that generally, the plants and trees, they are not very advanced in Kṛṣṇa consciousness. Trees and plants are generally among the 8,400,000 species of life in a very low status of consciousness, although I personally heard Śrīla Prabhupāda on a morning walk tell to Bhaktisvarūpa Dāmodara Mahārāja in a scientific discussion that they were having that the trees and plants that are above, on the surface of the ground, are more highly elevated in consciousness, even though they are immobile; they are more highly elevated in their consciousness than even the moving creatures that are in the water, such as fishes and crabs. Still, compared with human beings, the trees' level of consciousness is rather low.

Śrīla Prabhupāda was telling like this in that section of Kṛṣṇa book, that generally it is understood that trees and plants are in a very low consciousness. However, by the association of Kṛṣṇa and Kṛṣṇa's associates, these trees and creepers became so much infused with Kṛṣṇa consciousness that they wanted to offer everything they had. By His association, by His touch, they immediately wanted to offer everything they had. Whatever they had: their flowers, their fruits, and their honey, incessantly dripping from their branches.

This same feature of advanced Kṛṣṇa consciousness is found in any devotee, what to speak of devotees as advanced as the gopīs in the mādhurya-rasa. Any devotee naturally wants to offer his very best and everything that he is all about, thinking that, "My offering should be accepted by Kṛṣṇa," and that, "My offering should be seen as valuable." That, "Kṛṣṇa should value my offering, too." This is natural. It is not a matter of regret, or it is not blameworthy, that the gopīs would be thinking that they are being neglected. Why only this one girl? Even though the gopīs may be having that transcendental womanly vanity which is fully centered on the consideration of augmenting Kṛṣṇa's varieties of transcendental pleasures, still Rādhārāṇī is quite aware of Her transcendental preponderance, just like the moon among the stars.

She gives expression to this self-awareness in the verse that I am just now going to read. This is Rādhārāṇī speaking: "Among all the cowherd girls of Vraja, Śrī Kṛṣṇa is particularly affectionate towards Me. This is celebrated by all the people of Vraja. I am not making this up! The reason His super-excellent love for Me is celebrated is because My love for Him is considered to be like Mount Meru, whereas the love of the other cowherd girls for Him is not even like three or four mustard seeds in comparison."

It's getting later and later! Today is Pūrṇimā and we have so many things to do—to finish our Cātur-māsa vrata and finish our Kārtika vrata and finish our Bhiṣma-pañcaka vrata. By the way, is anyone following the Bhiṣma-pañcaka vrata here?

I should mention that if you are following strictly according to the program that I presented to many of the devotees here, today this morning or sometime relatively soon, we are to drink milk. And then in the afternoon around four o'clock, the pañca-gavya is to be mixed.

Pañca-gavya means the five items from the cow. The cow dung, cow urine, ghee, yogurt, and milk, these are to be mixed together and to be taken around four o'clock.

After taking these mixed items at four o'clock, then you should give in charity to the brāhmaṇas and Vaiṣṇavas – whatever: mahā-prasāda, cloth, donation, these kinds of things – and then break your fast by taking sweet rice. Starting at four o'clock is the honoring of pañca-gavya, then you distribute the charity and break your fast, and then – thank God! – shave and all these things. It's time for me to shave! I am so happy that today has come so that I can shave up! All this has to be done before the sandhi-prakāśa time, or the pradoṣa. Pradoṣa means when the sun has set and the light of the sun is still remaining in the sky. All this has to be done before sunset, in other words. But if for some reason you want to shave and you don't have time in that small one hour to do all these things, then it is permitted to shave after the pradoṣa time, after the last ray of sun has left the sky. But during the pradoṣa time when Lord Śiva and His cohorts are traveling in the sky, one should not shave. If you can honor the pañca-gavya and distribute the charity and break your fast with sweet rice and shave before the pradoṣa period begins, then that is best. We have one hour. From four to five ten. Sundown is at five ten today – moon rise. If you don't have any sweet rice to break your vrata with – I am going to collect all the sweet rice from the mahā-prasāda table in a few minutes, and I can distribute it. But you will have to come to my room or send an agent to my room.

Anyway, let's try to finish this. There is so much

important discussion actually. We could probably go to at least two o'clock with this. We will try to finish before twelve. No, I got so many things to do today; I shouldn't even be doing this!

Where were we? Okay, so let's try to read quickly. "My dear girlfriends have not been enjoying the great festival of this fathomless ocean of ecstatic nectar ..." This is the sign of Rādhārāṇī's concern for others. "... but instead are burning miserably in feeling Our separation." Para-duḥkha-duḥkhī. You understand, para-duḥkha-duḥkhī?

"Why must this be, and what can I do about it?" Rādhārāṇī thought. "If He and I wait here a few moments, then My sakhīs will be searching all over the forest and will quickly catch up with us. Concluding thus, I said to Śrī Kṛṣṇa, "O Beloved! I am unable to go any further! Let us rest here for a little while!" She was saying this to give Her sakhīs a chance to catch up with Her so as to relieve their feelings of separation from Them. "But the crest jewel of clever lovers immediately understood everything about the thoughts in My mind. Therefore, He who is unparalleled in His extremely cunning nature, who is matchless in His ability to relish divine mellows quickly deliberated within His own mind."

Now we are going to hear Kṛṣṇa's reasoning for leaving the gopīs and His reasoning for leaving Rādhārāṇī also. Kṛṣṇa thought, "If I take Rādhikā with Me to wander in these gardens, then that will not make Me happy, because this Rādhā can feel the mental anguish of Her girlfriends in Her heart and thus She also becomes very sad. And on the other hand, if I wait here, then all those girls will catch up with Us and look at Me with crooked eyebrows, and they will lovingly chastise Rādhikā for a long time, lecturing Her in many different ways. If this happens, then the mood of tasting amorous mellows sports will be completely spoiled and they will all return to their own homes in a huff. Thus there will be no chance of enjoying the rāsa dance tonight."

The whole purpose of going out there is to enjoy the rāsa dance. "And if the rāsa dance is not performed with all these gopīs, then" – now listen carefully – "then the prankish prayer that Rādhikā previously submitted unto Me will not be fulfilled." Now we are going to get some insight as to why there even was such a thing as mahā-rāsa in the first place.

Rādhārāṇī had asked, "Beloved, can you simultaneously embrace thousands and millions of gopīs with Your two arms?" I might just add my own little purport here if you don't mind. Many times in different places in the ācāryas' literatures we will see how it is that Kṛṣṇa is mildly rebuked by the gopīs as being a brahmacārī. And Kṛṣṇa sometimes audaciously boasts Himself to be a brahmacārī.

But the gopīs know very well what kind of brahmacārī He is. So Rādhārāṇī is saying, "You say that you are a brahmacārī, but we know what kind of brahmacārī You are. A brahmacārī is supposed to be able to control his senses. If You think that You are such a sober and dhīra brahmacārī, real dhīra means that You should be able to control Your senses in the face of the provocations. Someone may keep himself aloof from the sense objects and claim to be able to control his senses, but real sense control and real undisturbed sobriety can be tested when You are associated with the objects of the senses. So I want to see how sober and undisturbed You are! If You can embrace millions of gopīs simultaneously with Your two arms, then You will be able to rightly prove Yourself!" She says further here, "I am desirous to see such a feat. If you would kindly satisfy my request."

Kṛṣṇa is saying, "First, I will leave Rādhikā's company for a very short while, thereby proving to the other girls this poor helpless girl to be faultless, while taking all the blame on Myself." Just see how kind He is to His devotees! "First I will leave Rādhikā's company for a very short while thereby proving," I am adding, proving to the other girls who were in hot pursuit and would otherwise storm off in a huff. In other words, the other girls won't blame Her. He is willing to take the full brunt of the thing on His own shoulders. "I will thereby remain obliged unto Rādhā and at the same time will cause all the gopīs to become affectionately concerned for Her welfare in every way after they find Her crying alone in the forest."

This is very important now. We are getting to some really nectarean stuff. "By beholding the boundless, incomparably burning fever of Rādhikā's feelings of separation for Me, they will all be drowned in the great ocean of sheer astonishment. This will cause them to give up their own love-pride and realize that only Rādhā is absolutely the foremost lover of all. These proud girls will see that just as Rādhā is outstandingly the best in the mellows of divine union, similarly She is also the best hundreds of millions of times over in Her feelings of separation. The conjugal mellow in supremely nourished by these two moods of union and separation. When the gopīs behold Rādhā's heart-bending condition of separation from Me, they will become embarrassed, considering Her to be the topmost of them all.

"After I left the gopīs, they indignantly said amongst themselves, 'Alas, now Hari is simply overwhelmed with lust, for He has left us all to go make love with Rādhikā even though we are more loving than She.' Then they became very upset and had cast much blame towards both of Us. But now, when they find Śrī Rādhikā terribly suffering alone in the forest and are scorched by the exalted pique of her blazing fire of loving separation, surpassing their own feelings of loving separation a million-fold, then the gopīs will consider their own love to be like insignificant candles compared to Her great flame. My desire is that there be unity established among them all, and in this way My wish will be fulfilled. Thus at the time of sporting for the rāsa festival, when they are dancing in a circular formation and they see Rādhikā brilliantly shining alone with Me in the center, then they will not be jealous of Her in the least. Just as people apply a pungent ointment to their eyes that stings and makes the eyes temporarily numb but which afterwards renders them clear and brilliant, similarly a well-wishing friend sometimes purposefully gives another friend apparent difficulty that later results in the enjoyment of a wealth of happiness." Hare Kṛṣṇa!

There is so much more! The thing is that even by getting a glimpse of the vast ocean of wealth of the Gosvāmīs' contribution to human society in the form of their literatures, we can get strong niṣṭhā on the basis of our appreciation for the incomparable philosophy and exhibition of the truths about Rādhā and Kṛṣṇa as given in the Gauḍīya sampradāya.

Śrīla Prabhupāda has always told that the only way to actually understand Rādhā and Kṛṣṇa in truth is to take shelter of the teachings of the Six Gosvāmīs. As it has been discussed here, you will see that what Kṛṣṇa is trying to do, just like he told to Nārada Muni, "If you want to impress Me, then take shelter of Rādhārāṇī! If you say that you want to love Me, then you take shelter of Rādhārāṇī. You direct your love for Me through the services of the lotus feet of Śrīmatī Rādhārāṇī."

In other realms, you will find that they first honor Nārāyaṇa and then, after having done the pūjā of Nārāyaṇa, they do the pūjā of Lakṣmī-devī. But in our Gauḍīya tradition, we approach Kṛṣṇa through Rādhā. In other words, we take the flower and place the flower in the hand of Rādhā and request Rādhā to please offer this flower to Kṛṣṇa and beg Her that, "Kṛṣṇa is Yours. You have the power to give Him to me. I am simply running behind You, crying out 'Kṛṣṇa! Kṛṣṇa!' Please be merciful to me and tell about me, recommend me to Your Kṛṣṇa." And because Rādhārāṇī is so kind, Rādhārāṇī will turn to Kṛṣṇa, not thinking of Her own transcendental pre-eminence, but She will tell to Kṛṣṇa rather that, "Here is your devotee. Please accept her. She is many times more qualified than me." Then on Rādhārāṇī's recommendation, Kṛṣṇa will place His loving glance upon the devotee, embrace her, sport with her, and fulfill every desire within the core of her heart to an unlimited, never-ending degree.

And the devotee will happily – on behalf of Śrīmatī Rādhārāṇī – play the transcendental role of a love thief, understanding Śrīmatī Rādhārāṇī's experience, knowing Her to be experiencing ten million times the happiness of Her own meeting with Kṛṣṇa by Her making the arrangements for Her friends to meet with Kṛṣṇa, all the while absorbed in the treasure of the service of Śrīmatī Rādhārāṇī's lotus feet.

So [weeping], in the land of Vraja we chant "Rādhe! Rādhe!" because we know that Rādhārāṇī is our everything in our all. The vraja-vāsīs don't think in any other way. Kṛṣṇa, we can take Him or leave Him [laughing and crying at the same time]. What do we care for Kṛṣṇa? As gopīs of Vṛndāvana, we don't want to make any more friendships with that blackish boy! We remain ever ingratiated and ever allegiant to the lotus feet of Śrīmatī Rādhārāṇī. Rādhārāṇī is the life of our life.

Today is also another rāsa-yātrā, and it is on this day that Lord Caitanya entered into the rāsa-maṇḍala. You may remember if you have read Caitanya-caritāmṛta, maybe it is there in Teachings of Lord Caitanya as well, that when Mahāprabhu left Purī to come to Vṛndāvana, He was experiencing ten million times the happiness of his residence in Purī. Just by making the effort to go to Vṛndāvana, by commencing His journey to Vṛndāvana, He would experience ten million times the happiness of his happiness of residing in Purī.

And when He actually came to Mathurā and bathed at Viśrāma-ghāṭa, He experienced ten million times that happiness! And then when He finally came to rāsa-maṇḍala at Vaṁśīvaṭa, He experienced ten million times, ten million times, ten million times His happiness of residing at Jagannātha Purī.

As a matter of fact, His ecstasies were so tremendous and uncontrollable that His servant Balabhadra was afraid that Mahāprabhu might meet His demise at any moment. So at a certain point, he begged Mahāprabhu, "Please, let's go to Allahabad for Kumbha-melā." And Mahāprabhu, understanding the inability of His servant to cope with the situation, mercifully agreed to leave Vraja-maṇḍala, although He really didn't want to. This shows how much more powerful, in the matter of augmenting the ānanda of Rādhā and Kṛṣṇa is Vraja-maṇḍala than Jagannātha Purī. Even though Jagannātha Purī is also considered to be a vipralambha-līlā-sthāna.

It is on this day that Mahāprabhu came to the rāsa-maṇḍala and experienced the pinnacle of His happiness on His tour through Vraja-maṇḍala. Many Gauḍīya temples celebrate this day in order to commemorate that event. It happens that it's the same day, but actually, this rāsa dance is not mahā-rāsa. Mahā-rāsa was on sarodiya-rāsa-pūrṇimā. This rāsa dance is called Śrī Kṛṣṇa rāsa dance, and this took place not at Vaṁśīvaṭa or in the area on the Yamunā's shore, but at Govardhana. And it's now two minutes after twelve. It's time to chant our Kāma-gāyatrī mantra.

Oh, the point I wanted to make is mentioned in Dhyānacandra's paddhati about the Kāma-gāyatrī mantra and the Gopāla mantra and also the Rādhā mantra and Gaura mantra. Dhyānacandra says that these mantras are rāga-mayī mantras. These mantras are actually meant to be chanted to augment rāgānuga-bhajana. Rāgānuga-bhajana means that they are chanted on the basis of a greed to attain the result of the chanting which is the lotus feet of Rādhā and Kṛṣṇa, the land of Vraja, and the prema-sevās of Śrī Śrī Rādhā and Kṛṣṇa in the land of Vraja as well as Gaura in Nitya-navadvīpa.

In this regard, I wanted to read something to you from Rāga-vartma-candrikā which is very apropos and which should be very clearly understood by all of us: "Devotional service to the divine couple Rādhā and Kṛṣṇa done strictly according to scriptural regulations in vaidhī-mārga results in attaining Goloka in Vaikuṇṭha." Goloka in Vaikuṇṭha means, as we have previously discussed, the Vaikuṇṭha, or the majestic realm of Vṛndāvana on the Goloka planet, where Rādhā and Kṛṣṇa are worshiped in awe and reverence. Furthermore that means – what does it mean in vaidhī-mārga? Vaidhī-mārga means under rules and regulations, under the order of guru, under strict regulative injunctions of scriptures governed by logic and reasoning. It is termed as a fear-based obligatory devotion as such. But there is a vast distinction between so-called devotion based on duty-boundedness and devotion based on loving service attitude.

Guru has given us the Hare Kṛṣṇa mantra and ordered us, "You must chant a minimum of sixteen round daily. If you don't, you'll go to hell!" or whatever – you know. "You must follow the regulative principles; you must chant your Kāma-gāyatrī mantras three times a day. If you don't chant the Kāma-gāyatrī mantras three times a day, then take off this brāhmaṇa thread." Like that. So the bhakta is shaking in his shoes and says, "Aye, aye Captain!" And he is feeling, just by having been obligated on account of having taken dīkṣā, "If you have taken dīkṣā and you don't follow the order of the spiritual master, then you get sinful reactions according to the Pāñcarātrika-vidhis." So therefore, I am going on with my snig-snig ram-ram. Or I am chanting my "midnight-three," all the way up to 3:30am in the morning, hanging on my brāhmaṇa thread, sometimes drooling. Or if we have our daṇḍa, and the daṇḍa is falling over and bonking someone on the head. I have seen that happening sometimes in the middle of Bhāgavatam class. We give him the benefit of a doubt that he was working very hard for Kṛṣṇa the day before. That's why he is so tired and can't stay awake in Bhāgavatam class.

So that's vaidhī-bhakti, or at least it's a semblance of vaidhī-bhakti. Anyhow, rāga-bhakti is of a different nature. We will finish reading this paragraph and then I will paraphrase the point I wanted to bring out, because we were discussing about the distinction between worshiping Rādhā and Kṛṣṇa in vaidhī-mārga, and worshiping Rādhā-Kṛṣṇa in rāga-mārga. There is a very interesting point. This is Viśvanātha Cakravartī Ṭhākura's book, and he is describing here that the same activities that are performed in vaidhī-bhakti are also appropriately applied in the performance of rāga-bhakti. And it will be seen just like in vaidhī-bhakti:

śravaṇaṁ kīrtanaṁ viṣṇoḥ
smaraṇaṁ pāda-sevanam
arcanaṁ vandanaṁ dāsyaṁ
sakhyam ātma-nivedanam
(Śrīmad-Bhāgavatam 7.5.23)

These activities are performed in vaidhī-bhakti, but they are also there in the matter of the performance of rāga-bhajana. There is a saying in America that, "Yours is not to wonder why; yours is but to do or die." That is the essential bhāvanā, or attitude, in the vaidhī line. But Viśvanātha Cakravartī Ṭhākura describes that if the apparent activities of vaidhī-bhakti, such as hearing, chanting, and remembering, are prompted by lobha, or greed, to attain the result of residence in Vraja, following in the footsteps of the vraja-vāsīs, association with and prema-sevā to Rādhā and Kṛṣṇa, then that vaidhī-bhakti is not vaidhī-bhakti at all! Although to a casual onlooker it may appear that a devotee is engaged in vaidhī-bhakti, but if his activities of chanting the Holy Names, worshiping the Deity in the temple, or cooking for the Deities, or cleaning the temple, or studying the scriptures, or attending Bhāgavatam class, attending maṅgala-ārati, performing saṅkīrtana by chanting the Holy Name congregationally, or going out on book distribution, or chanting your gāyatrī-mantram, or any of these activities of devotional service that a devotee may do,– if the activity is done prompted by the greed to attain a particular result, namely the destination of Vraja, the perfection of service to the feet of Rādhā and Kṛṣṇa, that greed based on a knowledge of the fact that these activities are rāga-mayī, or these aspects of devotional service or these mantram – Hare Kṛṣṇa mahā-mantra, Gopāla mantra, Kāma-gāyatrī mantra – these are rāga-mayī mantras which are meant to produce the result of attainment of the realm of Vraja.

If I don't know that the fruit of chanting Hare Kṛṣṇa is the attainment of Vraja-dhāma, then I may not be prompted to take inspiration to chant Hare Kṛṣṇa for the purpose of attainment of Vraja-dhāma. If my guru gives me only the mantra but not the conception behind the mantra, which actually assists in the matter of producing the real effect of the mantra, then my mantra chanting will only be relegated to the realm of vaidhī-bhakti.

But if by the mercy of Hari, guru, the Vaiṣṇavas, and the scriptures I come to know that the real purpose and the real effect, or fruit, of performing these devotional activities is the attainment of the realm of Vraja and I become inspired by that knowledge to perform those activities in a hot pursuit of the desire to get that fruit, then our performance of the Hare Kṛṣṇa mahā-mantra, our performance of our chanting of our Gāyatrī mantras, our performance of our saṅkīrtana, our performance of our Deity worship, our performance of every other aṅga of devotional service, becomes rāga-mayī. And it is not at all vaidhī-bhakti, but rather it is an aspect of rāgānuga-bhakti.

Viśvanātha Cakravartī Ṭhākura is mentioning that devotional service to the divine couple, Rādhā and Kṛṣṇa, done strictly according to the scriptural regulations in vaidhī-mārga, in vaidhī-bhakti, results in attaining Goloka in Vaikuṇṭha. The devotee's devotional mood is aiśvarya-jñāna. That means that the devotional mood is predominated by the knowledge of Kṛṣṇa's opulences as the Supreme Personality of Godhead. And due to that knowledge of His aiśvarya, or opulences, the devotee is prompted to adopt a reverential mood of awe and respect in his approach to the worship of Rādhā and Kṛṣṇa. Due to this aiśvarya-jñāna, the devotee has not actually embraced the real spirit of a vraja-vāsī who is compelled to see Kṛṣṇa as the dear beloved or the son, or the friend, or his master, as in the mādhurya-mayī-dāsya of Vraja-bhūmi.

In this situation, the difference between svakīya-bhāva and parakīya-bhāva remains indistinguishable to him. When a vaidhī-mārgī, one who is following the vaidhī-mārga, or vaidhī-bhakti, develops an intense desire for mādhurya-bhāva, he becomes an eternal associate of Queen Satyabhāmā in Dvārakā, serving Her and Kṛṣṇa in svakīya-bhāva with mādhurya-jñāna mixed with aiśvarya-jñāna. So if someone is aiśvarya-jñāna-mayī in his approach to Rādhā-Kṛṣṇa-vigraha, then he attains the Vaikuṇṭha-vṛndāvana on the Goloka planet, and if there is an admixture of mādhurya-jñāna with aiśvarya-jñāna – in other words, if he is mixed mādhurya-jñāna-mayī and aiśvarya-jñāna-mayī in his approach to Rādhā and Kṛṣṇa – then really he will not attain Rādhā and Kṛṣṇa.

Bhaktivinoda Ṭhākura says in one place that even if a devotee is physically residing in Vraja-bhūmi, and even if he is worshipping the Rādhā-Kṛṣṇa-vigraha in Vraja-bhūmi, but if he is not approaching that worship in his vraja-svarūpa, adopting the vanity of a vraja-vāsī in pure mādhurya-jñāna, he will not attain the realm of Vraja and the service of Vrajendra-nandana Kṛṣṇa and Rādhārāṇī, but either he will attain the maid service of Satyabhāmā or Rukumini in Dvārakā, or he may attain the service of Lakṣmī-Nārāyaṇa because in Vaikuṇṭha, Rādhā-Kṛṣṇa are in the mood of Lakṣmī-Nārāyaṇa in the Vaikuṇṭha-vṛndāvana realm of Goloka.

As a matter of fact, there is mention in one commentary that even if one wants to have the closest amorous loving relationship with Vrajendra-nandana Kṛṣṇa in the realm of Vraja, if within his bhajana he remains attached to elements of aiśvarya-jñāna-mayī devotion, following the mood of the queens of Dvārakā, if these elements are mixed into his consciousness, then even though he has the intention of attaining Rādhā and Kṛṣṇa in Vraja, it will not be possible for him to do so because the land of Vraja does not accommodate that type of devotional mentality. The devotee will be relegated to an inferior realm which is set up to accommodate those inferior bhāvas.

Here he is saying why it is that the vaidhī-mārgī who develops an intense desire for mādhurya-bhāva becomes an eternal associate of Satyabhāmā in Dvārakā in svakīya-rasa with mādhurya-jñāna mixed with aiśvarya-jñāna. This is because the particular devotional mood, aiśvarya and mādhurya mixed, prompts him to see Rādhā on an equal level with Satyabhāmā. In following the process of devotional service in rāga-mārga, however, the devotee is elevated to the highest spiritual abode of Vraja, where he/she resides as an eternal associate of Śrīmatī Rādhikā, serving Her in parakīya-bhāva and pure mādhurya-jñāna.

Anyway ... Gaura-premānandī – hari haribol! I am very grateful to you for allowing me to take up so much of your time. I hope that I have not been in any way, let's say, impudent, or let's say pretentious, in the course of our discourses. I am not in control of my speech, nor am I in control of my mind.

But I am praying at the feet of Śrīmatī Rādhārāṇī, Śrīmatī Anaṅga-mañjarī, and Śrīla Prabhupāda that my words may be representative of their desires to express something for the benefit of all of you. I don't come out and speak very often. I am rather a recluse. A recluse means that I live by myself. I stay in my room and I rarely come out except to make some humble effort to share my enthusiasm for performing saṅkīrtana-yajña. I am actually very fallen and unqualified in most respects, you know; still, for some reason, somehow or other, because of Pūrṇacandra Prabhu's request and because of your enthusiasm to hear something, whatever it may happen to be, I have been inspired to try to say a few things over the last few days. If you think that you have heard anything which is of any value, then please kindly keep it as a treasure in your heart and cherish it for your whole life.

Perhaps, if Kṛṣṇa so desires, we may get another chance to have similar types of kathās sometime in the future. Not tomorrow! I can't say when I will feel inspired to even attempt to give expression to anything from my side. You may be knowing that I rarely give classes around here. And they are not really like classes; they are more like seminars, discussing from ever-increasing angles of vision. So if I have committed any offense, I beg your forgiveness. Thank you very much! Hare Kṛṣṇa!

www.ingramcontent.com/pod-product-compliance
Lightning Source LLC
Chambersburg PA
CBHW060623310726
48982CB00003B/651

* 9 7 8 9 3 8 7 4 5 6 7 7 8 *